T0365947

A Promise Kept

REBA STANLEY

WESTBOW°
PRESS
A DIVISION OF THOMAS NELSON
& ZONDERVAN

WestBow Press books may be ordered through booksellers or by contacting:

WestBow Press
A Division of Thomas Nelson & Zondervan
1663 Liberty Drive
Bloomington, IN 47403
www.westbowpress.com
1 (866) 928-1240

ISBN: 978-1-4908-3760-4 (sc)
ISBN: 978-1-4908-3761-1 (hc)
ISBN: 978-1-4908-3759-8 (e)

Library of Congress Control Number: 2014909034

Printed in the United States of America.

WestBow Press rev. date: 06/25/2014

Dedication:

To: The Great I AM.

David:

It may have been odd to have met you while out with another, but on that summer evening over thirty years ago, the Lord knew it was time to introduce me to the one He had made for me: you. 1-4-3

❧ CHAPTER ONE ❧

Fumbling for the obnoxious sound that had invaded his dreams, Richard reached across the bed moving only the part of his body necessary to slap the button to make the noise stop. Five-thirty in the morning isn't a pretty time for most people to rise and begin their day, but Richard really didn't mind it. He was a morning person and liked to watch the world around him slowly wake up.

Sitting at the breakfast table, Richard admired the early March sunrise as he raised his mug of hot coffee to his mouth and took his first sip. This was a beautiful moment for Richard. There was nothing like sipping his coffee each morning while letting it gently awaken his senses. As he drank the dark liquid and ate a blueberry Pop-Tart, he looked through the mail he had laid on the table late last night after returning from a basketball game. He usually glanced at the mail before tossing it on the table, but not last night.

Bills, sale advertisements and an envelope from someone by the name of Janice Tensely lay in a stack in front of him. Who is Janice Tensely? Taking another drink of coffee and tapping the corner of the envelope on the table as if this would help reveal who this person was, he didn't have a clue.

The mystery was quickly solved as soon as he saw the letterhead: Hunters Lane High School Alumni Association, Janice Mayhew Tensely, President. Now it made sense. Janice Mayhew was his former classmate from his old alma mater. Unfortunately, Richard only vaguely remembered her. Without the yearbook, he doubted she remembered him. The last invitation he'd received had been tossed as soon as he saw the words class reunion typed in black bold letters on the white paper. At that time it had only been five years since the class of '92 walked across the gymnasium platform receiving their diplomas. A reunion sounded silly. The class hadn't been out long enough to forget anyone. Some were still in college. He had not bothered to respond let alone attend. In this letter Janice's words reminded him it had been twenty years since they graduated from high school. Richard found himself wondering where the time had gone and curious to how she had found him. Quickly answering his own question, he figured she had contacted his parents or siblings since they still lived in the same town.

Through the years, the names and faces had faded, except Adam Garrett's, his best friend for as long as Richard could remember. As he drank his coffee, Richard reminisced about his school days. Bringing a small smile to his face he could never forget the prank the two of them had played on the girls in their class in the eighth grade.

Their entire class had been pulling pranks on each other for several weeks while ignoring their teacher's instructions for it to come to an abrupt halt. The girls were leading the boys after a side splitting lunch episode. Payback was in order.

"This will be so funny. We'll teach them to prank us," Adam had told Richard and his other buddies.

The bell had rung and the girls walked out of gym class. They had all returned to the locker room when Adam and

Richard calmly walked by the girls' locker room door. Without looking inside, Richard opened the door just enough to let Adam quickly toss in with the spray nozzle taped down a pungent bottle of Curve cologne for men. When it hit the floor, it began fumigating the room with the manly aroma until it was completely empty. Immediately the sound of high-pitched screams that only young girls can make echoed in the hallway then quickly followed by them running out of the room. Thankfully, no one had been undressing. Richard and Adam walked down the hallway unaffected by the commotion holding back their laughter until it was safe to let it rip. No one suspected these two making them feel as if they had just pulled off the cleverest of crimes.

As memories came forth, so did faces he had long forgotten. "What was that girl's name?" Richard asked out loud to no one. "Candace? Karen? Caroline? Yes, Caroline something." Richard's memory took him back to a day when he had noticed a girl coming into the library as he was exiting causing him to nearly drop his books. Until that moment, girls were unnoticed. But this girl was different. She was the most beautiful girl he had ever seen. He found himself searching for her everywhere. He looked intently in the hallways, the lunchroom, the library, until he finally saw her at a pep rally. He would have sat next to her had it not been for her silly girl friends squeezing into a space where there was none. He did see her from time to time, but he never got the nerve to approach and speak to her. He didn't even know her name until the yearbook came out. Thinking of Caroline caused him to smile wondering where she is now.

Returning to the present and the invitation in his hand, Richard read Janice's explanation of why there had not been a class reunion since '97. It seemed most alumni just do not show up for reunions anymore, and therefore the association eventually dissolved. After years of unsuccessful reunions, many high schools were opting to have one big event every few years combining several classes together.

Having been out of school for twenty years sounded odd to his own ears. Richard rubbed his chin with his hand as his brain processed this information. He casually laid the letter down to continue with his breakfast and the rest of the mail. Noticing the time, he left his coffee mug and the mail on the table and left for work not giving the reunion another thought.

Richard Dunning, the middle child of Todd and Karen Dunning, lived in Atlanta, Georgia, working as the marketing director of a pharmaceutical company. The fairly easy four hour drive to his middle Tennessee hometown where his parents and siblings lived was limited to Thanksgiving and Christmas due to his work schedule. He would make additional time if his niece or nephews were having a big event in their live or an emergency occurred. Otherwise, he was in Atlanta working and living his life.

Standing five foot ten inches tall with a medium build, Richard received his fair share of looks from the ladies. With hazel eyes, thick brown hair and his flashy, pearly whites usually got him a second look. But so far Richard had not met a woman he would want to spend every day of his life with. Until he did he enjoyed his bachelorhood.

Richard was successful at his job. He loved marketing, and it paid him well. His four years of college earning his degree had led him to a few jobs in varied locations. Currently he worked for Spade and Clyde Pharmaceutical Company. Being a very likable guy Richard rarely had problems with co-workers or clients, but there were days his boss made Richard's job tough. Joe Topmiller was successful without doubt, but too opinionated for Richard's liking. He wished he had known this before taking the position four years ago. But Richard had a plan. His goal was to earn some serious money, gain extensive experience and then move on to a position where he would stay until retirement. Up to now, it was running smoothly.

Parking in his usual space in the company parking lot, Richard mindlessly began his working day. After clocking in on his computer, he checked his messages and schedule noting how many phone calls he needed to return and what appointments he had before lunch. His daily phone calls were a major part of what put his job in motion. Today, overloaded with too many phone calls that he would somehow manage to make and three appointments spread throughout the day, he picked up the phone on his desk and punched in his first contact number of the day.

"Hello, Renée. You busy?"

"Rich, hi. I'm just getting my day started, so now is a good time."

"Great, perfect timing. Are you busy this evening? I thought if you weren't we could catch a movie. Maybe some dinner."

"Sure, that sounds good."

"I'll see you around six. Will that work for you?"

"Six is good. I'll see you then."

A beautiful young lady, Renée Bennett stood about five foot six. Her medium build categorized her as neither heavy nor skinny but rather the perfectly sized woman. With auburn hair and brown eyes, she attracted many young men. Unfortunately they proved to be more often than not wrong for her.

Richard and Renée ended their conversation and he quickly left to make his first appointment. He and Renée were just friends in his mind. They called each other several times a week, went out to dinner and to movies, and occasionally caught a ballgame. From this their relationship could easily be misinterpreted by any onlooker.

Brian sat at his desk looking over the books of his family's business. Todd Dunning had built a respectable plumbing business from the ground up when he was a young man and had made a nice living at it. Three years ago, Todd had decided it was time to retire, enjoy the fruits of his labor and spend time with the missus. In his younger years, he dreamed of the day he would turn his business over to his sons and give them a good start in life. Todd didn't want them to struggle as he and Karen did when they first were starting out. But his dreams didn't really pan out the way he had planned.

Richard, the elder of the two boys didn't stick around after college to step into his father's footsteps. He wanted something different. At that time he was unsure of what he wanted, but he knew he didn't want to work the rest of his life plunging out people's toilets and tubs. His brother Brian liked the thought of taking over for his father one day. That was his dream, but not Richard's.

Richard and Brian had worked with their father on weekends and during the summers while growing up. They knew the business inside and out. They could fix almost anything and take out any pipe ever made. Their sister Kathryn, Katie to family and friends, spent many summers behind the desk of their family business learning every inch from that angle. She also picked up a thing or two about a leaking faucet and a running toilet. After Brian took over for his father, he was confident that Katie would come back and work with him. She could run the company as well as anyone. He loved working with his sister, but she had a different career that she loved more than life itself, being a wife and mother. She filled in from time to time when needed without complaint, but her heart was elsewhere.

About six months ago, Brian saw an opportunity that had stuck in his head. He dreamed of taking his father's medium-sized plumbing business to the next level by turning it into a very large plumbing company with several locations in the middle Tennessee area. He knew it would take a lot of work and planning, and he knew just the right man to help him achieve that goal. However, getting Richard to come on board could prove to be a huge hurdle. Also, Brian felt he needed his father's blessing to go forward with his plans.

"Hi, Dad. What brings you down here today?"

"Oh, I have a slow day and didn't want to piddle around the house. So I thought I would come here and piddle around," Todd said with a smile.

Brian was actually glad his dad stopped in. He thought this would be the opportune time to introduce his expansion plans.

Todd sat quietly and listened to his son explain what he wanted to do. He actually had similar thoughts years ago, but felt it was too late in the game for him to take such a risk. As soon as Brian started talking about bringing Richard in, Todd's facial expression revealed frustration.

"He's made his choice. He doesn't want to work in the plumbing business. Now leave him alone," Todd sternly instructed.

"But, Dad, that was years ago. I think he may give it some consideration once he hears what I have in mind." The discussion went on for a while longer, but the result was the same.

"That was a good movie," Renée said breaking the silence as she and Richard walked out of the theater toward Richard's truck.

"It was. I love action superhero movies, but only if they are done right."

Renée laughed at Richard's words. "Well, of course. No one would like any movie if it were not done right." This caused them both to laugh.

Richard and Renée stopped at the Mellow Mushroom for a pizza. It was busy, just like most nights. The waitress quickly seated them and took their order. While their sausage and pepperoni pizza was being prepared, their conversation was light.

"I have tickets for the Atlanta Hawks game Saturday, want to go?" Renée asked.

"Sure, I love a good game on a Saturday, or Sunday, or Tuesday or…"

"I get the point, Rich." Renée chuckled. She knew Richard was a big sports fan, but didn't know his favorite. "Richard, which sport do you like best? I mean, you seem to really enjoy them all."

"True, I must confess. I love 'em all, well, except tennis. I mean, where is the excitement there?" Renée could not keep from laughing out loud.

Renée enjoyed sports more than most women. Growing up with brothers, she really didn't have much choice when it came to watching TV.

"Aah, here it comes," Richard said seeing their waitress coming their way.

Renée began putting pizza on their plates and their discussion about his love of sports continued.

"To be honest, I think I may like basketball the absolute best….that or hockey." Again laughter filled the air.

Monday morning began poorly for Richard. He got to work at his usual time and performed his typical routine when Mr. Topmiller called for a meeting of all the employees excluding the receptionists and secretaries.

Looking at the quarterly sales reports upset Mr. Topmiller and caused him to overreact almost every time. Joe Topmiller had been the General Manager for Spade and Clyde for the past seventeen years. The company joke was he had forgotten what it was like to actually do any real work for another person.

He started the meeting spouting off last quarter's report percentages and comparing them to this quarter's. The more he spoke the more his voice escalated.

"You people have gotten lazy. I will not employ lazy people!" Joe then turned to the sales manager Bruce, pointed his finger at him and gave him a direct order. "Bruce, no days off and no vacations for anyone until this little problem is corrected. Maybe that will get you people motivated," Joe said with heated firmness as he slammed the reports on the table. "And if anyone threatens to quit, LET'EM!" On those words, he turned and left the room.

Bruce stood looking where Joe had just stood hating that his boss just threw him a curve ball and then left the room. Now it was his job to smooth things over, to settle these people down and get back to work. He looked around the room at each face knowing not one of them was slacking off. It was just the recession. When the economy went down, so did the numbers. But somehow they would work through it. They always did.

After a few minutes, Bruce adjourned the meeting, and everyone left the room except Kyle Allen, one of the best sales representatives Spade and Clyde employed.

"Bruce, I'm sorry but I'm outta here man," Kyle said, extending his right hand to be shaken. "I don't need this. My numbers are always high. I give way too much to this company as it is. I'm in here for ten to twelve hours a day, five days a week. And because numbers are down, I get my days off and my family's vacation taken away." He shook his head. "That's not happening."

"I tell ya what. Don't make any decisions right now. Take the day off and think about it. I know after a few hours everyone will calm down, and we can get back to normal business around here. I'll talk to Joe and hopefully things will be better tomorrow."

Kyle agreed to not make a final decision at that moment out of respect for Bruce, but his mind was made up. He was done with Joe Topmiller and this company.

Richard sat alone at a fast food restaurant eating a chicken sandwich and some fries thinking about what had transpired in this morning's meeting when his cell phone rang. Looking at the screen, he saw it was his brother.

"Hi, Brian, what's up?"

Brian rarely called Richard in the middle of the day. Both men were too busy for idle talk during working hours. That was saved for when they both had free time.

"Hi, Rich. Just wanted to say hello and see how things are going for you. So, how's it going?" There was a brief moment of silence between the brothers and Richard wondered the real reason for Brian's call. Before Richard could comment, Brian continued. "Look, Rich, I'll get to the point. I need to talk to you about something. I want to make some serious changes in the company, and I really need your input."

"Why? It's your business. Have you talked to Dad?"

"Yes, I have, but, Rich, it's more than that. Don't get me wrong. Business is going well, but I do need to talk to you, ok?"

"Sure. I tell ya what. I really can't talk right now, so I'll call you tonight around eight. How's that?"

"Sounds great. I'll talk to ya then. Later, Rich."

Richard finished his sandwich, but could not keep from wondering what was going on with his brother.

First thing Tuesday morning, Kyle respectfully let Bruce know he was not coming back, and now he had to tell Joe the news. He hated this situation. It was Joe's arrogance and overbearing attitude that had caused this to happen. Bruce had tried to smooth things over, but fixing this was impossible. Joe had cost himself another good employee.

Bruce and Joe had worked together for seventeen years. Joe entrusted him to handle meetings and other company issues without much involvement accept when numbers were down. Bruce was well aware when this happened that Joe would be in the meetings giving his motivational speeches with tips to turn those opportunities into sales.

"I talked to Kyle this morning, Joe. He felt you went way over the line on this one. Said he doesn't want to spend his life working in such an environment." Bruce didn't tell Joe everything Kyle said, but he did want Joe to know he had been the one to cause this unnecessary problem.

Joe let out a loud sigh as he sat behind his desk and rubbed his forehead. He knew what Bruce was telling him was true. He sometimes did go over the line, and it had cost him good employees in the past, and now another one. But he would never admit that to anyone, not even Bruce. He had to stick with what he had said or he would lose control of the office. He was willing though to make this one exception where Kyle was concerned simply because he was one of his top sales reps.

Joe got Kyle's number from his secretary and punched it in while Bruce was still sitting in his office.

"Kyle, Joe here. Listen I want to apologize for the way things went in our meeting yesterday morning. You're a good employee and I would hate to lose you. I've reconsidered and am letting everyone have their vacations as normal."

"Thank you, Joe, I appreciate that, but I'm not coming back. I have other options I want to explore." Kyle said as little as possible to avoid burning his bridges.

"So, you won't consider coming back?"

"No, sir."

With that, Joe offered Kyle his best wishes and hung up the phone. Joe was the type of person who could get mad and scream at someone, and ten minutes later it was over, and to Joe, that is what this situation was: over.

"Hi, Chelsea. How are you?" Richard asked his sister-in-law.

"Hi, Rich, I'm fine. What have you been up to?" They chatted for about fifteen minutes before giving the phone to her husband.

"We really are doing a lot of business Rich, but I want to expand, start bidding on contracts for new construction, buildings and homes, that kind of thing. I've thought long and hard on this, Rich. And I was wondering if you would consider moving back here and help me run things."

"What would I do, Brian?" Richard said with a hint of a chuckle.

"You're the best marketing guy I know. You could do the marketing and all the bidding, things such as that. And I will oversee contracts, the laborers, field work and anything else."

"I don't know, Brian. I would have to give that some thought. I thought things were going well with you running the business by yourself."

"They are, but I think I can make us bigger and make more money, but I cannot do it alone. There's new construction going on all around me, and I want to get in on the action."

The two brothers talked at length about such a major change, but Richard never gave Brian any hint of an answer to his question.

The next few weeks were a blur for Richard. He had worked a lot of overtime and brought in a lot of business for Spade and Clyde Pharmaceuticals. He and Renée had not seen each other in over a week, but it couldn't be helped. All of this would pay off eventually, he was sure of it. With his list of clientele, he was always hearing of new business opportunities. He knew it would be foolish to leave considering how much money he was making now. He would stick it out a little longer.

With all the overtime Richard had put in, he was looking forward to a relaxing weekend of doing nothing. When he and Renée spoke over the phone on Friday morning, he explained that starting at five o'clock that evening he would be missing in action until Monday morning. While walking out to his truck he sighed, relieved that it was the end of his week.

Richard could feel the stresses of the week start to melt away as he made a mad dash to his neighborhood grocery to pick up a few necessities for a bachelor's weekend: frozen pizza, hamburger patties, chips, cereal, and plenty of Coca-Cola. He was beginning to feel guilty about not seeing Renée much lately, but he needed this time to himself. He wanted to sit on the couch all day in his sweats and T-shirt, watch one ballgame after another and not have to think about another person. He needed to unwind. He planned to do just that alone in his man cave.

Saturday morning, Richard's eyes popped open without the help of an alarm clock, and it felt good. Finally deciding to get out of bed, he grabbed a bowl of cereal and went through the week's mail that had piled up.

Before noon, Richard made sure he had all the items needed before the games began. He collected the remote control, the biggest glass he could find filled with Coca-Cola, and a large bag of Lay's potato chips. Without permission, the conversation with his brother came to mind. Knowing he needed to call Brain and tell him something, at this moment he didn't want to think about any business nor make any calls. Richard thought about Brian's offer, but he really didn't want to move back home and work with his brother. Quickly pushing it out of his mind when the game came on the TV screen, he got comfortable and didn't give it another thought. He was a little late wishing he had turned off his cell phone when he heard the first sound of its ring. Looking at the number to see if he could get away with not answering, he realized he couldn't.

"Yeah, man."

"Rich, hi. I'm in Atlanta not far from your apartment. Is this a good time or are you busy?" Adam asked.

"No, come on over."

If there was another male on this planet that loved sports as much as Richard did, it was Adam Garrett. Within ten minutes, Adam walked into Richard's apartment quickly noticing the basketball game and took the chair closest to him. Neither man bothered to talk until a commercial came on.

"What brings you to Atlanta?"

"I had to bring my brother to meet a friend. His truck is busted. It's a long story," he said with a wave of his hand. "It was sort of last minute, so while I was here I thought I would stop in and say hello."

"Well, last minute or not, I'm glad you stopped by."

"I also have these." Adam reached into his pocket and pulled out two tickets to a Hawks game.

"Oh man, where did you get those?"

"My brother. I guess you could say they're a little thank you gesture for driving him down here." The two men smiled at each other. The tickets were for the seven o'clock game that evening, and both men were as excited as little boys in a toy store.

Around five-thirty, Richard and Adam left for Phillips arena. On their way, he thought of Renée who too loved a good basketball game. The tickets weren't his to offer and there were only two. Sharing his good fortune with her would probably sting a little considering he announced his need for a weekend to himself. A Hawks game with a buddy wasn't exactly solitary. At times his friendship with Renée left him unsure how to act with her. Most relationships with women often confused him.

With hot dogs and drinks in hand, the guys made their way to their seats. Third row center court. To these two guys there was no better seating. Ten minutes before the ref blew the whistle, Richard turned his phone off and put it in his pocket. The two men did their share of talking during the drive to the game and while waiting for it to start. But after the whistle blew, the only conversation was the occasional game commentary.

Late Sunday night with much dread, Richard set his alarm and turned off the light on his bedside table. His mind replayed the weekend. He had enjoyed his time alone doing only what he wanted. He admitted with a tinge of guilt to himself that he actually wasn't alone and was thrilled that his friend had stopped by offering the tickets. Rubbing his face as he rolled over getting comfortable he noticed how good it felt not shave for two days and even considered growing a beard. Richard drifted off to sleep thinking about his great weekend, and as expected the alarm sounded before he was ready to be awakened for a new day.

Two weeks later, Richard got a call from his sister Katie telling him about an accident with their brother and her husband Russ.

"Last night Brian and Russ were on their way back from Springfield, and Russ said two deer jumped out of nowhere right in front of them. Brian swerved and tried to miss them, but hit one, which caused him to run off the road and flip the truck twice."

"Whoa, are they alright?" Richard asked seriously concerned.

"Well, Russ has a few scrapes and bruises, but Brian has a broken leg and collar bone. They are preparing him for surgery now."

"Are Mom and Dad there?"

"Yes, they've just arrived. Momma wanted me to call you. Rich, there really isn't any reason for you to come. She just wanted you to know what was going on."

"I'm glad you did. Call me when he comes out of surgery. I'll try and give him a call tomorrow. I know he won't feel like doing any talking any time today."

"You're right. He will probably be off work for a while too. You'll have time to catch up then."

"Umm, not being able to work for a while is not going to go over too well."

"No, it isn't."

Katie and Richard spoke a few minutes longer. She filled him in on more details of how the accident happened and a few other less serious family matters.

As Richard hung up the phone, he knew there was no way Brian would be at work any time soon. He also wondered how flipping a truck could cause one person to get seriously hurt and the other to receive nothing but a few scrapes.

Running his hand through his hair, he quickly began to calculate in his mind how each of the family could pitch in and cover for Brian, conveniently excluding himself. He was in Atlanta. He couldn't possibly leave his job to go and do Brian's. There was nothing he could do from here.

❧ CHAPTER TWO ❦

Caroline Martin worked at Vanderbilt Hospital in the ER admissions office which was more of a cubicle than an actual office. Today it had been busy. She saw many patients admitted for surgery, a pregnant woman with her frazzled husband and couple of kids, and one young man with a bad case of something. The worse case though was a young man who had gotten his hand severely cut on a table saw which made her cringe. As she sat typing in the information, she realized it was one of her son's friends causing her to almost jump out of her seat. After finishing her typing and inputting needed information into the computer, she left her cubicle to go see him.

"Dillon, what happened?" Caroline asked, trying not to show her shock as she saw the young man lying on a gurney with a bloody towel wrapped around his hand. Dillon's father looked like he was handling it much better than she would have.

"Oh, hi, Mrs. Martin. I got my hand caught in a table saw while I was helping Dad do some work."

"Well, sweetie, don't you worry about a thing. We have some of the best doctors around here that can fix that right up for ya. I'll see what I can find out for you. Do you mind if I let Joshua know you are here?" Both Dillon and his dad agreed that would be great if she would let him know and thanked her for her help. Caroline's shift was almost over, but she let them know she would check on them again before she went home.

Joshua and Dillon were juniors in high school and had been friends since the fifth grade. Dillon had been working around saws and similar equipment since he was about ten years old. Caroline couldn't help but wonder how this could have happened. Within twenty minutes, Caroline was back in Dillon's room explaining to them which doctor would be seeing him and letting him know that he was in good hands. She could not miss the obvious look of relief on both of their faces.

Normally Saturday was one of Caroline's days off, but occasionally she did have to pull a weekend shift. This was one of those occasions. Joshua had been with his grandparents all day with two of his cousins and she was hoping to beat him home. But the busy day ending with a stop at the grocery to pick up tonight's supper allowed her to only beat him by five minutes.

As soon as Joshua came through the door, he went straight for the fridge, as he almost always did. Grabbing the milk and then a handful of cookies, he noticed his mom coming into the kitchen. Taking one of his cookies, she asked about his day.

"It was fine. I helped Papaw with some stuff out in the building. Then he took me and Max fishing, but Michelle had to come too. She kept annoying me all day. Mom, why do girls do that?"

"What was she doing to annoy you? Other than wanting to be with her big brother and to do what you and Max were doing. It's normal for younger siblings to want to go and do what their older sibling does. Trust me."

"You did that to Uncle Curt, didn't you?"

"Noooo. Be patient with your little cousin, she can't help but want to have fun like you and Max do," Caroline answered leaving the room with a mouthful of cookie. Turning quickly around, she remembered her son's friend. "Oh, I almost forgot to tell you. You will never guess who came in the ER right before I left. Dillon. He cut his hand on a table saw."

"Whoa, I talked to him yesterday right after school. He said he couldn't hang out this weekend because he had to help his Dad build something." Joshua got out his cell phone and started tapping in numbers. Within ten minutes the plan was for he and his friends to meet and ride together to Vanderbilt to see Dillon.

Wiping her hands dry from supper preparations, Caroline picked up her ringing cell phone.

"Hey girl, what's up?

"Hi, Melissa. Just cooking supper. What about you?" Caroline answered.

"The same, but I called to ask if you have decided if you were going to the class reunion or not. I want to get my schedule planned out. I thought you and I could go together. Alex hates these things."

With a smile Caroline responded, "Alex isn't the only one." The two talked about the event at length mostly Caroline listening. Melissa had the gift of gab and today she was in rare form.

"I doubt I'll go," Caroline said when she got the chance.

"Oh, come on. It'll be fun! We can scope out all the popular kids and see if their looks have held up." Melissa started laughing at her own joke. However, the laughter stopped when Melissa learned that Caroline didn't want to go because she didn't want the reminder that most everyone else would be with their mates, and she would not.

Melissa quickly apologized to her dear friend. After all these years, she sometimes forgot that Caroline was a widow. Letting the matter drop, she assumed there would be plenty of time for Caroline to change her mind and plenty of time for her to help change it if needed.

When Richard got to work, he opened up his email to find forty-three unopened messages. He was sure only about half of those were worth opening, but there was one that quickly caught his eye. Adam had sent him a message.

Hey Rich. I keep forgetting to ask you this. Did you receive an invite to our high school reunion? Or did they forget all about you? Just kidding. I think I'll go. Who knows it could be fun seeing everybody again. Are you going? Adam.

Adam was always quick and to the point, his e-mails weren't any different. Richard chuckled at his friend. In reality he had forgotten all about the invitation.

Richard responded back to his friend.

Hey, Adam. When you coming to Atlanta again? I think I can get us some Hawks tickets, maybe not as good as the last ones you got…just say the word. As far as the school reunion goes, I really haven't given it much thought. Right now my mind is cluttered with work. Brian flipped his truck and broke his leg and collarbone. I may be coming for a short visit, but will let you know for sure. Be talking to you soon.

Richard's day was planned to the fullest. He had four appointments and little time for anything else. He quickly went through his phone messages and sorted them into two stacks: important and can wait. As he was picking up the phone to return his first call, Bruce called everyone into his office. Grumbling between his teeth how he had no time for this, Richard had exactly thirty minutes before he needed to leave for his first appointment.

"Guys, before you all get started with your day, Joe wanted me to call everyone in here and go over a few things," Bruce explained. Joe came in just as Richard looked at his watch knowing there was no way he could make his appointment if he stayed for this meeting.

"Joe, I have an early appointment. I really need to leave in about fifteen minutes," Richard quietly explained as Joe walked by him.

"Call and push it back a little."

"I can't. I've been working on this guy for six months." Richard felt Joe's solution was rude and would not even consider it. He had a scheduled meeting with an important potential client and he could not waste one moment of his time.

"What I have to say won't take long."

That response did not make Richard feel better.

Joe Topmiller rambled on for twenty-five minutes when it could have been wrapped up in ten. Unfortunately, there was no getting up and walking out on Joe. That would be disastrous.

As soon as Joe finished, Richard bolted out of the room tapping in numbers on his cell phone.

"Mr. Morris, Richard Dunning. I am so sorry I'm running late. My boss called a meeting right at the last minute. Please believe me, I tried and could not get out of it."

"Mr. Dunning, I thought you understood that I had a limited amount of time to give you this morning. I was here ready to do business with you."

"I know, sir, and I'm really sorry. I'm on my way now and should be there in ten minutes."

"It was by chance you got on my schedule at all this month. I think we should just call this one busted, Mr. Dunning. I have to be in another meeting in twenty minutes and I really don't think you can get here to talk this thing through in that amount of time. Feel free to call my office and try to re-schedule for another time."

"Yes, sir, thank you. And again, I apologize." The two men hung up.

"That's it!" Furious, Richard turned his truck around and headed back to the office. With quick and purposeful steps, his legs eating up the floor beneath him, he went straight to Bruce's office demanding he join him in Joe's office now. Not giving Bruce time to answer, he turned and walked out the door and down the hall to the big man's office.

Richard tapped on Joe's door but didn't wait for him to answer before walking inside.

"Joe, I want to talk to you. I hope you don't mind because this is important and this conversation is taking place right now," he said with a seriousness that could not be missed.

Bruce followed closely behind Richard, and the look on his face, revealed nothing good. Neither man took a seat as Richard began.

"A few weeks ago you called all of us into the conference room and yelled at us for our numbers not being as good as they have been. In your anger and frustration, you took away vacation time and days off and lost a good person because of it. Today I had an early appointment with Mr. Ronald Morris, Head of Atlanta Medical Associates. I've been working him for six months and I finally got an appointment with him. He told me up front his time was limited, and you took that time away from me." Richard paused for a brief moment. Joe opened his mouth to say something, but Richard cut him off. "I told you I had an important appointment and didn't have time to sit in on your last minute meeting. You cost me an important client and you cost me money. I cannot continue to do business this way, Joe. Consider this my resignation effective immediately."

Bruce was a little slack-jawed. Joe, however, tried to calm Richard down, but failed. He even tried to turn the situation around to make his actions look right and important, but again to no avail. Comments went back and forth while Bruce stood listening to both men. Finally, Richard walked out. Once again, Joe's actions caused another good employee to quit. Bruce stayed in Joe's office wondering if now was the time to give his opinion because he certainly had one.

Bruce immediately considered the impossible task of raising numbers with two less sales reps knowing that Joe was to blame. He had no time to hire new employees and even less now that his workload had just hugely increased. He wasn't happy about the entire situation. It made him feel like quitting himself, but he knew he could not do that. He had too many years under his belt with this company.

Back at his desk, Richard began clearing his belongings. He would cancel all of his appointments after he left the office. He needed to leave that building as soon as possible.

Richard stepped inside his apartment, set the box from the office on the table, then left to retrieve the mail. As he headed to the mailbox, he realized it was too early for the delivery. His thoughts wondered to what his next move would be. He did have options remembering the job offers he had turned down in the past few months. He would contact these companies again in the next few days to see if they were still interested. This naturally returned him to Katie's conversation realizing that he was now free to help Brian.

Richard called Katie and told her his news about now being available to help out their brother while he recovered.

"I don't mean this in the wrong way, but this is perfect timing, Richard. Brian needs your help badly. He will not be able to return to work for awhile," Katie assured him.

"It will give me time to regroup," he told his sister, hoping she did not hear the frustration he was attempting to hide.

"Well, just remember little brother, you're welcome to stay here with us. Just let me know."

"Thanks, Katie."

Their conversation was short. Richard asked his sister to pass the word around of his arrival. He really didn't want to spend the time calling Chelsea and his parents. He needed to pack, which made him think of Renée. With a sinking feeling, he knew he should call her and let her know he won't be around for a while.

"You quit your job?" Renée said slowly. "Do you have any leads to another one?"

"Actually, yes I do. I have a few clients that have offered me jobs lately. The question is do I want one of those positions?" He knew talking to her would help him sort things out as it usually did. Renée was a great listener.

"I'm sure you'll find something soon."

Richard's savings account could support him being out of work for a good while, but being unemployed too long would not look good on his résumé.

"I do have something…temporary, that is." Richard told her about his brother's accident and how he would be laid up for several weeks.

"And now that I have the time, I think I should go and help out. If I don't, my Dad will, and I really don't want him to do that. Since I know a lot about the business, I can step in until Brian is back on his feet."

Renée was happy Richard was helping his brother, but sad that he would be leaving Atlanta. She would miss him.

With a couple of bags in the back of his truck, Richard left Renée's apartment at one-fifteen Saturday afternoon. He hated long mushy goodbyes and wasn't going to have one now.

"I'll give you a call tomorrow."

There were days when Renée wondered exactly what their relationship was, but feared if she broached the subject he would run like a scared rabbit. She was certainly not ready to be without Richard Dunning in her life. She had no idea how she was going to deal with him leaving even temporarily. Fighting back the tears, she gave a smile that did not reach her eyes and nodded her head.

Richard reassured her he would be back in a few weeks and asked her to get his mail and watch his apartment while he was gone. After their small hug goodbye, Richard left Renée and Atlanta.

❧ CHAPTER THREE ❧

Richard made several stops along the way with one being in Manchester, Tennessee. He could not resist stopping at the Russell Stover Candies store. Every time he made a trip back home, he had to stop at that store.

Pulling into the parking lot, he knew showing up with a bag full of chocolates would make his sister one happy woman. Katie loved chocolate like no one else he knew.

Smelling the chocolate as he opened the door made Richard want a piece for himself. He casually walked the aisles wanting to see all the options before he made his decision. After making a second pass through, he finally selected some dark chocolate coconut clusters and a box of assorted truffles. He would be awarded as the best brother in the world without a doubt. Quickly walking over to the counter where a large display of hand dipped nuts, pretzels and other goodies lay behind the glass counter, he added to his cart a batch of chocolate covered almond clusters. Surrounded by all the delicious aromas, he was in the mood for ice cream. After ordering a large cone for himself, he paid for his treats and got back on the road.

Richard arrived at Katie and Russ's home in Goodlettsville in a reasonable time of five hours stopping only for gas, food and chocolate. He could have made it in a little less, but felt it wasn't necessary. There was already one Dunning son banged up, the family didn't need another.

∞

Katie let out a squeal when her brother held out the white bag with Russell Stover Candies stamped in brown letters on it. She was like a little girl getting a special treat. He gave the rest of the family their gifts as well, but their reaction was nothing like Katie's. It warmed his heart every time.

After supper, Russ and Katie filled Richard in on the details of Brian's recovery. Right now the man was not doing well.

"He seems to be in a lot of pain," Katie explained. Richard planned to go visit him before the hour got too late. "I told him and Dad that you were coming to help out. That seemed to give him some relief."

"Well, let's hope I can be of help. It's been awhile since I've worked in any area of plumbing. Katie, I may need your help to get started."

"Sure thing, little brother," Katie said as she began to clear the table.

Richard did visit with Brian that evening. Just as Katie had said, he was in pain and seemed to be on edge. Richard sympathized with his mood. After all, he had something broken on each side and at both ends of his body. However, Brian was relieved to have Richard come to manage the business while he was laid up.

"Katie's agreed to come in the office Monday morning and help me get my bearings. Dad was going to, but Mom wouldn't let him out of his dentist appointment," Richard said with a chuckle.

"I'm glad you're here, Rich," Brian said as he laid his head back for a moment. Richard took that as his cue to leave. It had been another tough day, and Brian was fading fast.

Monday morning, Katie brought Richard up to speed on the office routine, the employees and the shortage of plumbers. Over the past couple of weeks, two plumbers had quit and his receptionist left for maternity leave making them shorthanded. Two days before his accident, Brian had to fire a guy for his continual tardiness, and most importantly, for leaving a job before its completion which now left him short three plumbers. Rubbing his chin, Richard asked Katie how Brian ran a business this way. She explained the reasons were unexpected situations except for the receptionist; Brian had begun the search for replacements, but with the accident that search came to a halt. And how he forgot about a temporary replacement for Brook, she had no idea.

By two o'clock, Richard was torn between priorities, diving into the business end or strapping on his tool belt. He was never as thankful for Katie as he was today. The phone rang almost constantly, but she handled each call professionally and with ease. Unfortunately, she had to leave the office at two-thirty to pick up the kids from school leaving Richard alone to deal with all of it. He quickly decided if he needed help he would call his dad.

"Tomorrow, I can only be here until noon. Dad will come in and help when I leave," Katie said as she gathered her purse and keys and told him when supper would be ready. "I hope he can do as good of a job as you." Katie just smiled at him and went out the door.

Now wading knee deep into the family business, Richard wondered why Brian seriously wanted to transition this small operation into a big one when he was having such labor issues. If it weren't for the desperate situation caused by the accident, he would not be dealing with it. The books were in great shape and Dunning Plumbing was turning a profit, but it appeared Brian had problems keeping good workers for long periods of time.

Brian spent the whole day being cranky and in pain. When he was not in pain he was either dozing off or sound asleep. He wanted badly to be at work with his brother, but he knew he would not be of any help. He wanted to interview potential new employees, but in his condition he couldn't even answer the phone or set the appointments. He felt totally useless. For the past several months, he thought continuously of turning his small business into a thriving large one. Now, here he lay in bed with broken bones and a broken spirit. He spent a lot of his days sleeping due to the medication, which he didn't complain about. He figured if he was asleep he wouldn't think of his condition. But when he was awake, he was miserable.

Chelsea had to wake her husband for supper. She had been cooking his favorite foods the past couple of days hoping that would help his mood. So far the effort didn't alter it, but this evening it did.

Richard called Brian right after the meal was over to report on the day and ask a few questions.

"So, what do you do when you are short on plumbers?"

"I do the job myself. Just because I'm the boss doesn't mean I don't go out there and unclog a few drains." Richard was hoping he wouldn't have to do that. "I've already placed an ad in the Tennessean and spread the word around at the hardware stores. We should get a few bites any day. Dad can help with the hiring. I can't believe I forgot that Brooke was going on maternity leave. How could I be so stupid?"

Richard felt a little more informed after talking to Brian. It had been a while since he did any serious plumbing work, but he could do it. If he had to, he would put the tool belt on. His first priority though would be to add a few good workers on the payroll.

A week later, Richard was meeting himself coming and going. He appreciated his Dad and Katie's help, but it seemed most things had to have his attention. It didn't help that his cell kept ringing.

If Brian called Richard one more time, he was going to throw his cell phone in the trash. Richard was busting his behind getting his brothers business back on track, so why wouldn't he leave him alone and let him do just that. It had been a little over a week since Richard had taken over for his brother and thought all was going as well as it could. But now Brian called about every hour and it was driving him nuts.

"That's it!" Richard said as he tossed his cell phone on the desk. "Dad, make him stop!" Richard stood in front of Todd with his hands on his hips and fury in his eyes. "I cannot deal with him any longer. How does he expect me to get anything done with him calling all the time?"

Todd knew Richard was at the end of his rope, and Brian was just not himself lately. The family had been bending over backwards to help make things easier for him for which Todd now saw was making things worse.

"I'll talk to him, son."

Todd left the office to go speak to his younger son. He always told his children to never put off dealing with something unpleasant if you can, because everything else will be unpleasant until you do. Todd prayed in his mind as he drove from Nashville to Goodlettsville to Brian and Chelsea's home. When he arrived, he asked his daughter-in-law if she had any errands she needed to run. "I have to talk to Brian about some stuff at the office," assuring her that it was nothing serious. Chelsea took advantage of the opportunity.

"Brian, I'm going to the grocery while your father is here. I won't be long," Chelsea whispered to Todd on her way out the door, "Actually, Todd, you are doing me a big favor. I needed some time away from this house." She kissed him on his cheek and went on her way.

Todd walked in the living room where Brian sat in his recliner dressed in lounge pants and a Nashville Predators T-shirt with his left leg propped high on a pillow, and right arm in a sling. After chatting a few minutes about his recovery status, Todd got down to business.

"Son, I don't want you to call Richard anymore. You are driving him nuts." Todd was also not one to beat around the bush. "He's working his tail off trying to help you while you're laid up and he can't get anything done for you calling him every few hours. It needs to stop."

"What do you mean I'm..."

"Now, hear me out," he said, holding up his hand. "You wouldn't put up with that and neither should he. The only reason it's me here telling you this instead of him is because he is upset right now. And I don't want the two of you going at it and getting all mad at each other." Todd picked up Brian's cell that was sitting on the end table beside his chair and held it up as he continued to speak.

"I could take this cell phone with me and not give it back until you're back at work. But then I suspect you would make things a little harder on Chelsea, and we cannot have that," he said, emphasizing the word cannot.

Todd and Karen had noticed Chelsea looking tired lately and assumed it was Brian running her ragged. "I'll have Richard call and report to you every few days if you just have to know what's going on. But it would be best if you trust your brother and let him deal with things while you're laid up. Don't forget I'm there most of the time and I ran that business for years without any help from either of you. You are not going to be like this forever son, but it is going to take some time to heal."

Brian did not take his father's words well, but realizing he was being a nuisance, he agreed to stop calling his brother and wait for Richard to call him instead.

Todd made the drive from Goodlettsville to Nashville in about half an hour. Walking into the empty office, he could hear Richard on the phone. Hearing the conversation, he knew Richard would be leaving to pick up some needed supplies. Todd could see the fatigue and frustration on his son's face.

"Son, It's almost quitting time, so why don't I go get those on my way home and you call it a day?"

"No thanks, Dad. I need to talk to those guys anyway. I figured I would ask if they knew of anyone needing work."

After all the aggravation of the day, especially Brian's endless phone calls, Richard was enjoying the drive. He passed a Sonic and decided a milk shake would do him a world of good. As he finished ordering, his cell rang. Reluctant to answer, he looked at the screen before answering it.

"Yeah, Dad?"

"Son, I forgot to tell you, when you go in the store, ask for Melvin. He knows what we usually order almost as well as I do. He's also the one you'll want to ask about any out-of-work fellas."

"Thanks, Dad, I'll be sure to ask for Melvin." Richard ended his call and sucked up the last of his strawberry shake with a few extra slurps. The sound was almost embarrassing to his own ears. "Aaahhh, that was good."

Pulling up to the hardware store he noticed they were fairly busy for a Thursday at this time of day. A small and friendly older woman asked if he needed any help as soon as he stepped inside the doorway.

"Yes, ma'am, I need to speak with Melvin. Is he available?"

The woman picked up the phone and paged Melvin to the front desk. Within minutes a tall man with gray hair and a bushy mustache walked up to the counter.

"Yes, sir, can I help you?"

"I'm Richard Dunning from Dunning Plumbing and I'm ..."

"Yeah, Todd Dunning. How is that old coot?" Melvin quickly assumed this young man was Todd's son, seeing that he was the spitting image of a younger version of the man.

"He's fine, ornery as ever. I'm here to pick up some supplies. My brother Brian usually places the orders, but he had an accident a few days ago, so I'm filling in."

Melvin got caught up in the story and the resulting injuries, then quickly guided Richard to the back and pulled up their records on the computer to view their last order.

"Now, I have thread tape sealant here on the shelf, but I'm out of drain sticks. They're on order. It should be here in a couple of days, but we can deliver those to you so you won't have to make a special trip down here." Running his hand through his hair, Richard gave the helpful assistant one more item. "Melvin, I also need a couple of keys made."

"Alright. I'll get those for you. It won't take but just a minute."

The employees at the hardware store didn't sit or stand around. Everyone who worked there kept busy with something.

"Hi, Rodger, how are you?"

"Hello, Caroline, I'm fine, what can I help you with today?"

"I need two sets of these keys made," she said holding two keys separately from the others on her key ring. "And my bathroom sink is clogged, again. I thought I would try that stuff you sold me the last time and see if that fixes it. Do you remember what that stuff was?"

"Sure do. Follow me. You know you may need to have that looked at since it keeps acting up."

"I know, but I thought I would try to fix it myself first. A plumber is not within my budget right now." As the two walked to the aisle where the liquid sat on the shelf, she remembered that was not all she needed to pick up. "Oh, I almost forgot." Reaching into her purse, she pulled out a few links of chain showing it to Rodger. "I also need this type of chain for my daddy's porch swing."

Caroline and Rodger were talking about her sink issue as they approached the back counter where he would cut the chain for the correct length and make her keys. Richard stood leaning into the counter as he waited for his keys. He couldn't help but overhear their conversation and certainly was not going to reveal that he was running a plumbing business or that he could easily fix her problem. Not until he saw the face that went with the voice, that is. As the sound of her voice came closer to him, he could not keep from turning his head toward the sound. Seeing only the female who had been speaking, Richard was almost slack-jawed at the sight of the prettiest woman he had ever seen. Her beautiful figure reached about five foot four with stunning light brown hair. She could have easily been a model for shampoo products.

The woman laid her keys on the counter as she opened her purse and placed the sample pieces of chain back inside. Richard just happened to be on her left side and noticed, as her pretty hand moved gracefully; she was not wearing a wedding ring.

"Excuse me, ma'am. Did you say you were having trouble with your sink?"

Caroline looked at this man with the most beautiful blue eyes and answered. "Yes, but Rodger has what I need," she said with a kind smile, and then turned away. Richard almost missed what she said due to those eyes. How could Rodger be so calm helping a woman like that?

"I'd be glad to help you. I run a plumbing business here in Nashville."

"No, thank you. That won't be necessary." Caroline looked Richard's way only when she spoke directly to him briefly making eye contact, then quickly turning her head away.

"Are you sure? I really could fix that for you, and it probably won't take very long." He could not understand why this woman didn't jump at the chance for a plumber to come to her rescue and fix an irritating problem.

"Again thank you, but no. I'm sure this will do the trick." Turning her head toward the store employee and receiving her items, Richard knew their short conversation was finished.

"Rodger, make sure you tell your wife I said hello." On those words, Caroline turned and walked toward the front of the store to pay for her things.

Rodger never spoke a word. He just left Richard standing across the counter with a bewildered look on his face as he watched this woman walk away.

Richard was a little dumbfounded by what had just transpired. It wasn't every day you visit the hardware store looking for a temporary fix on a drain problem, and find a plumber standing there right next to you offering his help. Well, be that way, he thought.

On her way home, Caroline did not allow Mr. I-can-fix-that-for-you to invade her thoughts. It irritated her when someone just butted in on her conversations and tossed their expertise on her. But with the help of the radio she tuned it out. Mindlessly pulling into the driveway, she saw two other vehicles parked in front of her house.

Joshua and his friends had been to see Dillon. Caroline opened the door to find Joshua, Eric, Heather, Austin, and Jana sitting around the table snacking on chips and Pepsi. She didn't mind. Joshua's friends were always welcome in their home, unless they got unruly, which had never happened.

"Hi, guys, what's up?"

"Hi, Mrs. Martin," the group said in unison.

"We've just got back from seeing Dillon," Joshua explained.

"How is he?"

"He's doing better."

"You should have seen it, Mrs. Martin. He has a lot stitches." Eric explained.

"Yes, that was cool," Austin said.

"Cool? How is almost cutting your fingers off cool?" she replied.

"Getting cut was not cool, but to see it. Now that was cool. I mean all that inside stuff that you never see. I think I may want to be a surgeon some day."

This caused the group to laugh out loud. Austin was the one who always said the funniest things unintentionally. His friends were not laughing at him in an unkind way. It was just funny in an Austin kind of way. Another reason for the humor was that Austin and anything academic requiring deep, intense study simply didn't go together.

"No really, I mean, when we saw him in the hospital before they fixed him up, he let us look at his cuts. We saw the inside of his fingers and part of the inside of his hand. I actually saw the bone, Mrs. Martin. Or wait a minute, that may have been a tendon," Austin said as he was getting his cell phone out of his pocket. "Look, I took a picture of it. Wanna see?"

"No. Thanks, sweetie, I'm…I'm good."

"Yeah, Mom doesn't like looking at the insides of bodies," her son teased.

"He's going to be out of school for a couple of weeks 'cause his medicine makes him sleepy. So we have offered to help with his homework and stuff so he won't get too far behind," Jana answered.

"I think that is a wonderful idea. I'm sure he appreciates that."

After Joshua's friends left, Caroline told her son how proud she is of him and the others. They were going the extra mile to help a friend. "That's true friendship."

❧ CHAPTER FOUR ❧

This particular week proved to be trying for everyone. Since Brian no longer called his brother several times a day, it meant Richard needed to call every few days to update him on everything. He still had not hired any new guys, but had three interviews lined up for Monday morning. Richard had to go out on a job himself late Friday afternoon not finishing until well after supper. He pinched his finger with a pair of needle nose pliers bringing a blood blister that deserved respect from anyone who saw it. Tired and hungry with his back aching, he was ready to throw in the towel. After a week like this one, Richard's mind was made up. The moment Brian recovered he was going back to Atlanta. He would not continue working with his brother at Dunning Plumbing. No matter how much Brian begged, he was going home.

Brian's healing was progressing as the doctor predicted. He wasn't in as much pain now, but his patience was running thin. He had slept so much during the day in the last couple of weeks that he no longer could sleep through the night giving him and the others a new irritability to deal with.

Todd and Katie were taking turns coming in to help Richard with office needs. They all agreed not to hire a temporary receptionist until after Brian returned. Todd could not do the payroll with the new system Brian was using which left Katie with the task. Somehow the bookkeeping had fallen behind and could not be put off any longer. If she stayed and finished it, she would be late picking up the children. To prevent interference with car pools and supper preparations, she brought the work home and created a mini office space in the dining room. Working on the payroll and the evening meal caused Katie to forget about Jake and ball practice. Turning off the stove and quickly grabbing her keys, she and the kids ran out the door. "Ashley, sweetie, I'm sorry you'll just have to do your homework during ball practice."

Realizing the meal she attempted to make three and a half hours earlier was now ruined, she decided it was burgers and fries on the way home.

"This bed has never felt so good," she said to her husband, crawling under the covers after midnight. She was tired, but the payroll was done.

Caroline and Joshua were preparing for a three day school trip. On their way home she thought about the laundry needing to be done. Pulling onto her street, Caroline felt something odd happen to her car. Slowing down to a crawling pace, she continued until she reached her driveway. This action was unthinkable for most men, but she was not a man. As a woman and being this close to her house, she drove on and would figure out the problem when she arrived. After pulling into her driveway and getting out of the car, she immediately found the problem. "A flat," she whined, suddenly feeling thankful it was only a flat.

Joshua was carrying a load of clothes to the washer, when Caroline walked in the house. His favorite jeans were not clean. This wasn't a problem for him, but knowing his mother, he knew she would ask him point blank if he had packed clean clothes or those that had already been worn.

"Joshua, sweetie, I have a flat tire. How about I do that and you take a look at my tire before it gets dark, please? Oh, and that little air pump is in the trunk.

"Not a problem. I'd rather air up a tire than do laundry any day."

Caroline finished loading the washer while Joshua looked at her tire. There had been many times she wondered what she would have done if the Lord had given her a daughter instead of a son. Who would do those man jobs that women could not do or should not have to do? "Thank you, Lord, for giving me a son," she softly whispered.

Joshua told his mother he saw what looked like a roofing tack in the tire. "If we leave early enough tomorrow, we can stop by Jack's on the way to school. I'll have him remove the tack and plug it." Caroline always took her car to Jack's Auto for repairs. He was a little pricey, but honest about his work. "I'll tell him what we need so you won't have to go in."

Caroline smiled at her son, "I think I can handle that part."

"I know, but I don't mind. I'll do it." Caroline saw almost a pleading in her son's eyes at that moment. So she let the matter drop. The truth was Joshua didn't want his mom dealing with manly responsibilities that other moms didn't have to. Auto shops were one of them.

∞

Monday morning seven a.m. Richard grabbed a cup of coffee and began reviewing the resumes for the upcoming interviews later in the day. He had three scheduled before lunch and was determined to hire someone on the spot.

The first candidate proved to be a total waste of time, and Richard was trying not to show his frustration. The young man was late and didn't represent himself well. He appeared to be unorganized and had worked in three different places in the past eight months.

Richard felt confident about the second interview and thought would be a good addition. Afterwards decided he would suggest to Brian they offer this man the job today. At eleven o'clock, Katie informed Richard that his final interview of the day had arrived. Something sounded odd in her voice, almost a hint of humor.

"Ok, show him in."

Richard's back was toward the door as he was putting away a folder in the filing cabinet when it opened. Richard turned around and assumed that Katie had not yet sent in his next appointment as she said.

"May I help you?"

"I hope so. I'm here for an interview."

Richard caught his jaw dropping open and quickly closed it. Having an office that was mostly windows toward the rest of the building, Richard saw Katie give him a big grin.

"Aah, yes, of course, I'm sorry." Looking at the résumé again and reading the name Sidney, he automatically presumed Sidney was a male. He was clearly mistaken.

With a little too much bleach on her hair and big brown eyes, Sidney Reese stood about five foot seven. She wore snug khaki pants and a pink button up blouse that needed to be buttoned up a little higher. Her shapely figure attracted second looks from men, but after closer inspection her hands were not the hands of a delicate woman. They were not thinly shaped with long polished nails, but actually short and stubby with a bruise under the nail of her left index finger. Richard had to make an effort to make sure he looked at her eyes and nowhere else.

At first, Richard's mind was made up. He would not hire a woman plumber, especially one that looked like her. But she knew plumbing and needed a job as desperately as he needed to hire someone. Richard proceeded as he did with the other two. He was determined to not treat her any differently just because she was a woman. He wasn't prejudiced. As the interview went on, Sidney proved she knew as much about plumbing as any man he had talked to.

"Ms. Reese, please forgive me, but I have to ask. Why in the world would you want to work as a plumber? I mean, it is not a glamorous job," Richard asked as politely as he could.

"No, Mr. Dunning, it isn't, but it does pay well. My husband left me two years ago for another woman. I was barely making it. And when things around the house broke, I could not afford to have them fixed. So I learned how to fix things myself. Later I started taking classes online for what I already knew how to do. Now I have a piece of paper saying that I know how to do the work. I need this job, Mr. Dunning.

I know plumbing is not the best job for a woman, but like I said, it pays well and I know how to do it. If I didn't, I would not be here wasting our time."

"Well, I'll be honest with you, Ms. Reese. We've never had a woman plumber work here before, although my sister can hold her own when it comes to a leaky faucet."

Richard didn't like the sound of his own words nor his thoughts that seemed to come on their own ambition. A woman working as a plumber was unconventional. His thoughts raced. Was it safe? Would men feel intimated by her? Would they hit on her while she was on a job? Would he get sued if he didn't hire her? And what if he had to fire her? Would he get sued for that? However, he knew if he did hire her, he would have Katie talk to her about appropriate work attire.

"I assure you that your gender will have nothing to do with you getting or not getting this job. There is one other person we are seriously considering. And when I say we, I mean my brother and I. I'm actually filling in for him until he gets back on his feet. He will be the one making the final decision. You should hear something by Wednesday, Thursday at the latest."

On those words, Richard and Sidney stood and bid each other good day. Richard had never been in this situation before. In all his years, he had never seen a woman plumber. If he had seen Sidney's ex-husband, he could say he had never seen such a fool either.

Sidney felt good about the interview. She felt she had a chance of getting the job. Showing up to work every day for a boss as nice and handsome as Richard Dunning would be the easiest thing she had ever done.

Brian took the idea of hiring a woman plumber fairly well. He had never considered it but had never had a woman asking him for a job as a plumber. Todd on the other hand shook his head in disbelief, "Times sure have changed." Before Richard left, all three men agreed to hire both Sidney and Rob, the second interview, leaving one more opening to fill. Overall, Richard felt the day had been productive which made him feel better.

Joshua and his classmates loaded the bus at eleven o'clock Thursday morning and left for their annual retreat to Hillmont camp. Everyone's excitement filled the bus with happy noise. The kids were talking, laughing and cutting up. The teachers didn't mind until it got too loud. Then Mrs. Raven asked if they would keep it down a little. Of course, this only lasted for about fifteen minutes. The other teachers tolerated the rowdy bunch because there was just cause for the noise. Mrs. Raven tried reading a book and would look up occasionally to make sure all was well while a few other teachers did as some students. They put in their ear buds and listened to music. Joshua and his friends sat near each other and played video games.

Caroline dreaded going home knowing Joshua would not be there. Being alone didn't bother her, but when he was away overnight, she felt his absence. She knew one day he would go to college then eventually leave permanently to start a home and family of his own. She would handle that when that time arrived, but for the next few days, she would visit her parents and Melissa and catch up on some reading to keep herself busy. She would be fine.

On her way to her bedroom to change clothes, Caroline passed her son's room. Glancing inside, she noticed his bed and let out a chuckle. Joshua had not bothered to take clean sheets with him as suggested by the teachers organizing the trip. He just took the sheets that were already on his bed and packed them. "Boys." After changing clothes, she put fresh sheets on Joshua's bed. Knowing if she didn't, he would put the ones he took with him back on. She stopped herself from picking up his room because he wouldn't like not knowing where anything was.

When she was alone, Caroline usually treated herself with eating in front of the TV. It was more about not feeling alone rather than a treat. Due to Joshua's messiness, she didn't allow him to eat in the living room unless it was a special occasion. She placed her plate and iced tea on the table beside her favorite chair and turned on Wheel of Fortune.

Melissa called and the two talked for an hour. She brought up the school reunion again. During the conversation Caroline realized Melissa really wanted to see her old classmates, but still wasn't sure why. She felt a little guilty about telling her no when her friend wanted to go so badly. How many places has Melissa gone with her just because she wanted to go. Remorse began to creep on her, so she told her she would think about it. Melissa was delighted to hear Caroline's words. "Great, we've gone from a 'no' to an 'I'll think about it'."

Richard had been away from Atlanta for three weeks and decided to spend the weekend in the comfort and privacy of his own home. His sister and her family made him feel very welcome and at home, but he needed some time to himself. He and Renée had either spoken on the phone or written an email two, three times a week. She would send Richard what appeared to be important mail each week and tossed what was definitely junk. He was appreciative he didn't have a pile of mail to go through when he returned.

Walking into his apartment, Richard could feel the stress from the past three weeks melt away and was looking forward to sleeping in his own bed. Of course, the fridge was totally empty except for a box of Arm & Hammer baking soda. So a trip to the grocery was imminent.

Picking up his cell, he tapped in Renée's number. Just as Richard was about to end his call, she answered.

"Well, what do you know, we finally connected." Richard and Renée had missed each other's calls for the past week.

"Hi, Richard. I'm sorry we kept missing each other. How are you?"

"Fine. I'm home…but just for the weekend. Can you come over this evening?"

"Uh … yeah, I think I can." Richard felt her answer sounded odd.

"Is there a problem? Are you busy?"

"No. I…well…I have to work late. So I probably can't make it before eight."

"That's alright, I'll see ya at eight then. Will you have eaten?"

"Yes, the boss is bringing food in, so there's a plus."

Richard and Renée ended their call. He then made his way to the grocery and for some takeout for one. Driving back to his apartment, he could not shake the way Renée sounded to him over the phone.

❧ CHAPTER FIVE ❦

It was eight-twenty when Renée tapped on Richard's apartment door. Quickly answering, Richard hugged Renée before she stepped over the threshold. He was thrilled to see her, and she him.

"You look great." Richard said as she walked on in.

"Thanks. I don't feel so great after working a ten-hour day."

Renée slipped off her shoes, and Richard poured her favorite cold drink as they eased right back into their old routine of kicking back with each other.

Something that had never happened to them before suddenly did happen. There was a moment of silence and awkwardness between them. Renée wondered if she was the only one who noticed. It had only been three weeks and they were struggling for things to talk about. This was not a problem over the phone or in email, but now, here face-to-face, words would not come.

When Richard left for Tennessee, Renée knew she would miss him terribly. The first few days were the toughest. But as the days went on, so did she. The two stayed in touch as always, they just weren't seeing each other. It was then she realized she was unsure about her feelings for him other than a close friend.

"Renée, are you alright?"

So he did notice, "Yeah, why do you ask?" Richard looked at her wondering about this sudden awkwardness between them.

"Has something happened that I don't know about? Or is something going on that I am oblivious to?"

"Richard, I want to ask you a question, and I want you to be totally honest with me…please?"

"Oookaaay."

Taking a breath and looking Richard directly in the eye, she needed to see and hear his answer. "Richard, what is our relationship?"

"What do you mean?" Oh no, wrong response. He would not blame her if she threw something at him for that stupid answer.

This sort of gave Renée her answer, but she continued. "What is our relationship? You know, what are we to each other?"

Richard was blindsided by this question. He would have rather avoided it like the plague. With every woman he had dated when he realized she was getting too clingy or wanting to get more serious, he ended the relationship. With Renée, it was different, they were pals he felt. Somehow he had missed those signs…until this moment. Now here he sat with alarms, bells and whistles going off in his head telling him to exit quickly, and her waiting for an intelligent answer.

"Aah, well, Renée, I think you and I are very good friends…close friends. We like hanging out together with no pressure of any kind. We know each other very well…we're… comfortable with each other."

Renée gave him a half smile and continued.

"Two weeks ago, I met this guy. He is a friend of a friend. Yesterday, he asked me if I would like to go with him to see a play next weekend. I told him I would have to get back with him, and let him know. If what we have is just a good friendship, then it should not matter if I go. But I really wanted to make sure you and I didn't have feelings for each other and neither one us telling." There it was she had said it. It was all out in the open now, or sort of anyway.

Renée's serious look was new to Richard. What was he to do or say? He liked Renée and was certain she liked him, but he did not really have romantic feelings for her. Could it be Renée had romantic feelings for him and this was her way of telling him?

"Renée, I think that we both need to be honest here. I care a lot about you, and I think you care a lot about me in return. We have a great friendship, and I don't want anything to upset what we have, but neither one of us has said or shown the other anything to cause the other to think differently. If you think this guy is all right and you would like to get to know him better, then you should go. But," he said quickly, "I hope this guy doesn't mind us being good friends and hanging out together. I found you first," he said with a smile and a pointed index finger in the air. Renée slightly smiled in return.

So it's just a friendship she concluded. At that same moment her cell rang. She was grateful for the interruption though she didn't answer it. She simply looked to see who it was. "Thanks Rich, I just needed to know where we stood. The last thing I want to do is hurt you."

She stayed for another hour, and then told Richard she really needed to get going. Not only was she physically exhausted from her long day at work, but now was emotionally drained and needed to be done all together. On her drive home, her feelings hovered between the sadness of knowing she and Richard would never be more than friends, and relieved that she and Richard would never be more than friends. She was unsure which was stronger.

The weekend turned out to not be what Richard had looked forward to. He felt he was losing someone dear to him without a way of stopping it. He did not see Renée again before he returned to Nashville, but did talk to her twice. She had to work half a day on Saturday and her brother had come to town for a few days. She assured Richard they would continue to keep in touch while he was in Tennessee.

The bus pulled up to the school parking lot early Saturday evening as Caroline and many other parents waited for the group to return.

Joshua and a few other guys helped unload the luggage from the bus making the tired teachers happy while speeding up the process. Of course, receiving extra credit for their manual labor gave them the incentive to be helpful.

"So, Mom, what did you do while I was away?" Joshua asked in a sing-song voice on the way home.

"Oh, I kept busy. How was your trip? Anything exciting happen?"

"It was fine." This was the typical answer Caroline knew she would hear. "Brittney lost her camera, then someone found it for her, then she lost it again. Mrs. Raven turned her foot, but she was fine by the next day. Other than that, nothing... oh, and on the way there the bus ran out of gas. That was funny."

"How does that happen?"

"Easy, the gas gauge on the bus doesn't work."

"I guess that's how that happens."

Caroline and Joshua stopped at Papa John's for pizza. Happy her son was home, she looked forward to a relaxing evening with a pizza and a movie.

As soon as Caroline and Joshua pulled into the driveway, so did Caroline's dad. He had told his daughter he would stop by and take a look at her sink. Caroline had already forgotten she had asked him to come and check on it.

For Caroline, Sunday mornings were the hardest day of the week to get out of bed. On that day the pillow never fit more perfectly, the bed never felt more comfortable and sleep was never more resting. Maybe the problem this Sunday was she and Joshua had stayed up until eleven-thirty watching a movie. Silently scolding herself for staying up too late, she only had time for toast and a glass of juice for her breakfast. Miraculously somehow, they were out the door and on their way to church on time. The parking lot was pretty full as usual. Adam and Sabrina pulled in behind her relieving Caroline and Joshua of being the only ones cutting it close this morning.

"Good morning. Oh, I'm glad I caught you. Are you and Joshua coming to the cookout next Friday?" Sabrina asked.

"I'm planning on it, and as far as I know Joshua will be there too." Joshua was already several steps ahead of his mother as he made his way to the door.

Music was being played softly signaling everyone to begin moving to their seats. The music at the Marydale Bible Church was second to none. The Lord's presence was evident. The pastor walked up to the podium after the song service ended to begin his sermon.

"It's so good to be in the house of the Lord today, amen?" Many voices could be heard echoing "Amen." Brother Whitehurst unbuttoned his suit jacket something he always did before starting to preach. "Let's all open our Bibles to the book of Mark and listen to what God has to tell us today." All across the auditorium you could hear the sounds of pages being turned followed by a sudden hush over the room. "Dear Heavenly Father, thank you for this day. Would you please bless the reading of your Word and help me to speak only the words you give me. In Jesus' precious name I pray, Amen."

"How are you doing on believing God these days? Are you ok, or do you find yourself lacking? I have to admit there are days when I'm ok in that area, but then something happens. And it may not necessarily be a major thing, but I will find myself lacking. What makes us go up and down on the belief scale? Let's read, shall we?"

"First, I want to read Mark the second chapter and starting at verse ten. This is where Jesus heals a crippled man. 'But that you may know that the Son of Man has authority on earth to forgive sins...' He said to the paralytic, 'I tell you, get up, take your mat and go home.' He got up, took his mat and walked out in full view of them all. This amazed everyone and they praised God, saying, 'We have never seen anything like this!' Now turn with me to the fifth chapter of John as we read about Jesus healing at the pool. Let's begin reading at verse five, 'One who was there had been an invalid for thirty-eight years. When Jesus saw him lying there and learned that he had been in this condition for a long time, he asked him, 'Do you want to get well?' 'Sir,' the invalid replied, 'I have no one to help me into the pool when the water is stirred. While I am trying to get in, someone else goes down ahead of me.' Then Jesus said to him. 'Get up! Pick up your mat and walk.' At once the man was cured; he picked up his mat and walked."

Brother Whitehurst continued, "Now, I don't know about you, but I'm thinking that both of these men here had to have a little bit of faith. They had to believe in the One that told them to get up and walk. Many times in our lives, things happen and we get knocked down and we cannot for the life of us get back up. Years ago, a friend of mine lost their only sibling in an accident. They were in a state of shock for a while, as any of us would be. And one day my friend said to me they felt as if they could not move forward. It was as if their feet were glued down and they could not take a step. My friend accepted Jesus in their heart many years prior to this event -- that was not the problem here. They knew that God was there the whole time. They knew that God did not make a mistake in taking their sibling home, but as the days, months and even years passed, my friend seemed to be emotionally unable to go forward with their life."

Brother Whitehurst took a pause for a moment before he continued, "Maybe you are like my friend and have lost a loved one, and you just can't get on with your life. Or maybe you've lost your job and you are struggling and cannot seem to get back on your feet. Maybe you have had something happen to you physically and you cannot walk. Or maybe, just maybe it's nothing as serious as these things, but it is something that has you down spiritually. You are crippled and cannot get up and walk away from it. For my friend, they could not get up and walk away from the hurt they felt inside. They could not get up and resume their life. Nor could they accept the fact that this had happened to their family and no one on this earth could fix that. No one could make that hurt stop."

"My friend forgot that Jesus heals all hurts. Jesus commanded the cripple man to get up and walk. And the man did not try explaining why he could not walk, nor talk the issue to death. He simply obeyed. His faith in the One who gave the order to get up and walk healed him. We think too much on our problems. And at times we think them into being bigger than they really are. Yes, the loss of a loved one is big, but nothing is too big for Jesus. He is sufficient for all our needs."

Brother Whitehurst closed his Bible and looked out over the congregation and began his closing comments. "So, I ask you today, what has you crippled? What has you down where you cannot get up and walk? Take that to Jesus and believe in Him to heal your hurt or struggle. He can fix it. It may not be the fix we want, but He can remedy our issues and cause us to get up and walk again. Listen. Listen closely, do you hear Him saying to you, 'Pick up your mat and walk?' Let's all just pick up our mats and walk."

Brother Whitehurst buttoned his suit coat and motioned for the music director to lead the congregation in a hymn of invitation. After the closing prayer, people began to mingle as they walked toward the main entrance.

"Joshua," Turning around to see Adam coming toward him.

"Hey, you're coming to the cookout Friday night aren't you?"

"I think so."

"Good, cause I need your help in getting a team together for some volleyball. Talk it up with the other guys and let's get as many as we can to come. Face it, Joshua, you're a leader amongst you friends, dude." With a chuckle Adam slapped Joshua on the back then turned to find his wife.

After a delicious Sunday dinner at her parents' home, Caroline changed clothes and made herself comfortable in her favorite chair she nestled in almost every Sunday afternoon while reading a book and enjoying a glass of Dr. Pepper. She was reading a remarkable book about a woman who had lost her husband after twenty years of marriage and who then found a second love of her life. This caused Caroline to think of her own situation wondering if it would have been harder to lose Craig after a lifetime of loving him versus only a few years. Of course she had no answer. She also wondered if you could truly love another man after loving one man with every fiber of your being and then losing him to death. That she doubted. She was convinced she would never love another man like she did Craig. Because of this deep love, she hadn't even considered going on a date in many years.

Two years after Craig's death, Caroline went on her first date. It was a disaster, or so she thought. They got along well and seemed to have a good time, but she felt like she was being unfaithful to her husband. Her friends had played matchmaker and knew of a 'great' guy for her. She discovered quickly he wanted a little too much too soon. Finally, she said no more. She was content with being single and didn't wish it any other way. After her last date with Mr. Wrong, Caroline had learned how to avoid men when she felt they may be interested. Now, many years later, dating or remarrying never entered her mind.

❧ CHAPTER SIX ❧

It rained the entire drive from Atlanta to Nashville Sunday afternoon which closely matched Richard's mood. He could not shake the conversation he had with Renée. He was unable to say they broke up because they were never really a couple. Neither one was upset at the other. They seemed to be fine when they spoke last, but Richard was definitely feeling down. He felt he had lost something dear to him. Missing his exit for Russell Stover's added to his gloom. With the events of the weekend going through his mind, he didn't even realize his error until five miles past the exit.

"How could things change so quickly?" Richard heard himself say out loud. "All was going well. My job was going well. I was making good money, I had a great friend, then bam! All of a sudden, no job, I leave my home to take care of my brother's business, and now, Renée is…I don't know what Renée is. And all within a few weeks. I don't even know where to call home anymore. I just. Don't. Get it!"

Richard pulled into his sister and brother-in-law's driveway about seven o'clock. He chatted with his family, played video games with the kids and then excused himself to his room. He really wasn't looking forward to going to work tomorrow. Katie would be there in the morning until two, and then their dad would finish out the day. With Chelsea's help Brian had done some research for a new bid on a project downtown and needed Richard's help with the details. "Aaaahhh!" Richard groaned as he rubbed his hands up and down his face and through his hair as he fell back on the bed.

∞

"Yes, ma'am, let me put you on hold for just a moment while I look at the schedule and see if I have anyone available this afternoon." Pushing the hold button on the phone, Katie looked around for her brother.

"Rich," Katie called to her brother as he was walking by.

"Yes, Katie what is it?"

"We need someone to go to Madison around four today, and everyone is scheduled out on a job but you and Dad. This lady needs someone to look at her bathroom sink as soon as possible."

Richard stood there wondering why the lady didn't just schedule an appointment. "Well…have her make an appointment like everyone else," he replied with a bit of confusion.

"She said her father talked to Dad last week about it, and Dad told him something to try but that didn't work and now it is seriously backed up. And she doesn't get home from work until four." Waiting a few seconds Katie asked, "What do you want me to tell her?"

"Tell her we will have someone out there after four o'clock."

"Ma'am, I'll have someone out there after four to take a look at it."

The day had been a busy one. At three that afternoon, everyone remained tied up at various job sites. Richard and

Katie were the only ones in the office meaning there was no one to make the service call to the Madison home.

"Rich."

"Yeah?"

"I think you're on deck."

"What?"

"There is no one to take that service call in Madison, so you're it."

Running his hands through his full, dark hair, Richard thought for a moment, then walked around to Katie's desk and looked at the work schedule. "Where did you say it was?"

"Madison."

He immediately thought of Sidney. Knowing she would do anything for him, he would call her to ask if she would like a little overtime pay.

"Hi, Sid, it's Richard. Listen I have a customer in Madison who needs help right away. Is there any way you can get to her this evening?"

"Well, Richard, I would love to help you out, you know I would, but I'm sorry I'm still going to be awhile at the Chambers home. And it's way out in Brentwood."

"Ok, thanks, I was just checking to see if anyone would be available soon." Ending his call, Richard rubbed his face knowing he was going to have to do this one himself.

Richard had gone on only one service call since stepping in his little brother's shoes. Since he was the temporary boss, he preferred his leadership role by assigning someone to do the job. Today it looked as if there was no other choice. All his workers were onsite with other jobs. He would feel selfish letting his father go just because he did not want to do it himself.

"I'll stop by there and take a look at it myself. Write down the address. I have a phone call to make first, then I'll head that way."

Living with his sister's family while his job situation was in limbo along with he and Renée speaking less frequently, Richard's mood was a bit sour. And now he had to deal with some woman with a stopped-up sink.

❧

Caroline had just walked in the house and laid the mail on the table when she heard a truck pull in her driveway. She looked at the time seeing exactly four o'clock and noted impressively the promptness.

"Hello, I'm Richard Dunning with Dunning Plumbing."

"Yes, please come in. My sink is acting up again. My father called and talked to someone about it last week. We've been putting a liquid down it off and on to unclog it, but the problem keeps recurring."

Richard didn't mean to stare, but he had seen this woman before, but could not place where. "Oh, I'm sorry," embarrassed to be caught staring. "He talked to my father, Todd Dunning...Forgive me, but have we met somewhere before?"

Oh please! She cried within "No, I do not think so. If you'll follow me, I'll show you to the sink and you can get started," Caroline said quickly to avoid the question and additional conversation. She figured if she avoided conversation answering only when needed, he would stop talking to her and just fix the sink. Caroline kept looking at her watch wondering why Joshua was not home. She really didn't like workmen or delivery men to be at the house when she was alone because she felt too vulnerable.

To Richard, this was not an average customer with a stopped-up sink. All of the sudden this was a beautiful mystery that intrigued him. No, he had seen her somewhere before because he could not forget a face like hers. He would figure it out eventually. Rolling up his sleeves, he began his work.

At four-fifteen, Joshua came through the door very aware of the look on his mother's face.

"Why are you so late?"

"I had to take a makeup quiz," he said with a defensive tone.

"Oh, that's right, I'm sorry," Caroline said putting her hand to her forehead sounding a little stressed.

"I see the repairman is here." Without responding, Caroline didn't want Joshua to know she was a little on edge from the man's earlier comment. Normally that would not have bothered her in the least, but it had never been said to her in her own home.

Joshua walked to where the man was working to see what all he was doing. He had drained the water out of the sink and was on the floor turning a bolt with a crescent wrench. Joshua wanted to know what he thought the problem was, but didn't ask.

"I've got to get something from the truck. I'll be right back," Richard said getting up off the floor.

Richard quickly grabbed what he needed from his truck and walked back into the house being careful not to track dirt on the floor. He learned early in life women didn't like that. Caroline was in the kitchen preparing supper. She turned away from the counter to set the table when she saw Richard walk back in.

He stopped after shutting the door and looked at her again. "Are you sure we have not met before? You look very familiar." Caroline didn't want to be rude by telling this man to stop asking her that, but instead kindly said no as she returned to her supper preparations making it clear to him that she was not interested in conversation.

While Richard was working on the sink, Joshua told him what they had done to fix this little problem in the past.

"We usually pour this stuff down the drain to open up the clog," and handed Richard the bottle.

"Where do you buy this?"

"Ace Hardware. It usually works, but not this time. Papaw thinks the problem is with the pipes."

Listening to the young man while he twisted and turned with all his strength, he finally loosened the trap. "I get most of my supplies there. It's good stuff, but the problem is ..." Suddenly, Richard remembered where he had seen this woman and it caused a small grin of victory to come across his face. "...Not so much with the pipes themselves but rather what is in the pipes. Sometimes things get dropped down the sink and get stuck."

Joshua's cell made a noise. After checking the caller, he left Richard to his work to reply to the text. He returned ten minutes later to see his progress. Sitting on his knees with one hand on his thigh and the other holding a piece of pipe as he studied it, Richard acknowledged Joshua standing in the doorway watching. "Like I said, sometimes things get stuck in the pipe. I pulled that out." Richard pointed to a disgusting glob of something with an earring sticking out of it laying on a piece of torn paper he had in his tool box. "This pipe is old and really needs to be replaced. See this spot right here?" he asked Joshua pointing to a spot on the pipe. "It's almost rusted through. I have a pipe on the truck that I think will fit which will eliminate the next problem."

"Well, this is going to be fun when I remind little Miss No-Thank-You-Only-Rodger-Can-Help-Me that I'm the guy who not only offered to help her in the first place, but also the guy who fixed it," he said to himself with attitude.

After replacing the pipe under the sink, he turned on the water to see if it went down easily, and it did. He then began cleaning up his work area. As Richard slowly put his tools away, he found this all so amusing. He was anxious to see how this little lady, who so quickly dismissed him weeks ago in the hardware store, was going to react when he told her where they had met. He planned to enjoy watching her face when she learned that the person she refused help from is the very person who came to her rescue. Suddenly, he remembered how beautiful she looked that day. Even now in her work clothes she was beautiful, but he figured it was best not to mention that.

Walking toward the front door, he saw Joshua sitting at the table eating his supper while Caroline was puttering around the kitchen. Richard sat his toolbox on the floor by the front door. Hearing him, Caroline turned and met him there.

"Your dad was correct. The problem was the pipe, and this," he said, holding up a shiny oddly shaped earring that he had extracted and cleaned.

"So that's where I lost it," she said, wiping her hands with a dish towel then reaching for the shiny object.

"I replaced the pipe and the water is running out easy. But if there's another problem just give me a call. You know, like in case you drop the other earring down the sink," he said, grinning as he wrote out the bill on a pad. It was then he made his move.

"I figured out where I had seen you before," he said, tearing off the top sheet and handing it to her. It was at Ace Hardware. You were in asking for something for this drain. Remember? I asked if I could help you, and you quickly said no thanks." He couldn't control the grin on his face. But seeing those beautiful blue eyes staring back at him, he almost forgot what he was saying, and his words came out kinder than he had planned. Somehow the victory lost its sweetness.

"Hmm, I'm sorry I don't remember." She was being truthful. But as she looked at him now, she felt a little embarrassed. "When in the hardware store, I just go to Rodger. He has been my hardware guy for many years. He takes care of my needs and then I'm out the door."

Lucky man he thought. "Well, Mrs. Martin, like I said, If you have any more problems just give me a call."

As Richard was driving home, he kept replaying his evening at Caroline's in his head. He really didn't know why, but it also kept him awake for most of the night.

Richard was up to his ears in work when Brian came in the office. He was looking at everything testing Richard's nerves. He was about to abandon ship when his cell rang.

"Hey, Rich. How's it goin'?

"Not well, Adam. What's up?

"Sabrina and I want to invite you to dinner Friday night. We're having the teens and their parents from our church over and would love to have you work your magic on the grill in return for food. Think you can make it?" Richard and Adam constantly joked with each other. Their strong friendship provided an open invitation into each other's homes and life no matter what. Today was no exception.

"Would it be too early if I come now?" Richard chuckled and told his friend how Brian was pushing his buttons today.

Brian had been at the office for two hours and his strength was fading. It frustrated him when he got so tired in the middle of the day.

"I'm outta here, man, you're doing a great job. Really, you are. Keep it up," he said as Chelsea wheeled his chair toward the door.

At four o'clock Richard called Adam and let him know he would not be making it after all. Turning down free food was rare for him, but it couldn't be helped. After spending several hours on the phone with their accountant, he was spent. Richard wanted to make sure Dunning Plumbing had the finances to build their business, which required extra time going through the books with their accountant.

∫ CHAPTER SEVEN ∫

Adam's eldest daughter Lindsey was one of the star players on her basketball team. Being a proud father, he and his family supported her throughout the season, which was now winding down. The build up towards the championships was intense. Richard was disappointed that this was the first game he had had the opportunity to see her play. He hustled to get there on time barely making it. Tonight's game was the Goodpasture Christian School Cougars versus the Donelson Christian Academy Wildcats.

Richard got to his seat with his popcorn and a Coca-Cola ready to see the game when he nearly choked on his first sip. He coughed a little staring in disbelief at the court.

"Adam, who is that?…The ref with the pony tail?"

Scanning toward where Richard was pointing, "Oh, that's Caroline Martin. She refs for a lot of the Christian school basketball games, mostly the girl's games. She's good too. Why?"

"Just asking. I did some work for her not long ago. I…I thought she looked familiar."

Caroline blew her whistle and called a foul on one of the players. Richard turned back to his popcorn, and watched every move Caroline made. He could not take his eyes off her. There she was in black slacks, a white and black stripped shirt, black shoes and her hair pulled back in a ponytail. He honestly didn't know how any male could keep his attention on this game.

The Cougars were up by three when Lindsey Garrett, number twenty, was fouled. Lindsey walked up to the free throw line to take her shot. Caroline handed her the ball with her whistle in her hand near her mouth. Lindsey readied herself and took her shot adding another point to their score. The game continued at full pace. Richard was trying to watch the players, especially Lindsey, but his eyes kept wondering to Caroline. He had never paid so much attention to a referee before as he did tonight.

Caroline never played basketball, but she watched it often with her dad, brother and of course her husband. After Craig died, she needed extra income. Doug Williams, a friend of theirs, worked on the side as a basketball referee. He led her to the right connections to learn how to become an official and she was now one of the best officials in the area. There were times she and Doug worked together, but she mostly officiated girl's games and preferred it that way. Occasionally, she was asked to officiate a boy's game and gladly accepted. When that happened, she appreciated working with a friend like Doug.

Joshua was about five years old when she first began refereeing. Her parents would watch him while she worked. Occasionally he would accompany his mother to the games, but had to sit next to the scorer's table. "Stay in this seat, and at half time I'll get you a hot dog or a hamburger," she would tell him, and he always obeyed. There were also times when her brother Curt or her dad would come to the games and watch Joshua. Since both of them loved basketball, neither one complained.

During the drive home, the game was fresh in Richard's mind. He kept seeing Caroline running up and down the court with the kids. "I cannot believe this woman. This totally feminine, beautiful woman…is a basketball referee," he said to himself.

Caroline had periodically invaded Richard's thoughts from the first time he saw her at the hardware store. But after working on her bathroom sink, she had almost taken over his mind. Before now no woman had impacted him like that. He imagined asking her out and her accepting. He envisioned them spending time together, but picturing this beautiful woman, as a basketball referee, never entered his mind.

Reality hit Richard square in the jaw. She clearly seemed uninterested when he was at her house. Of course not! What kind of a person acts interested in a plumber, especially one they have just met? He had to see this woman again, but clueless as to how and where. The man was overwhelmed with his thoughts.

It was the last game before the championship. If the Cougars won, they would be on their way. After discovering Caroline's side job, Richard made sure he was at every game following that night. He had only seen her at that one game, until tonight. He was determined to talk to her during halftime, or after the game, or both. She was not getting away before he had a chance to chat with her.

Richard's attempts to stay focused on the game were futile with Caroline as the ref. He loved basketball like nobody's business, but this woman distracted him. Instead, he just watched her. He almost stood up and nailed a guy for yelling at her for a call she made, but Richard kept himself in check. Finally the buzzer sounded and it was halftime.

Quickly leaving his seat, he walked to the scorer's table to say hello. He had no idea what he would say to her, but he was happy that his feet knew the way. She stood with the other referee near the scorer's table sipping water when Richard spoke more calmly than he felt.

"Caroline."

Turning toward the sound of her name, Caroline looked at him waiting for him to continue. This took her by surprise because usually fans didn't come up to the officials and talk to them during a game.

"Hi, Richard Dunning, with Dunning Plumbing... remember? I repaired your sink a few weeks ago," Richard said noticing a few men behind the scorer's table and the other ref looking at him oddly.

"Oh, yes, hi."

"I thought I recognized you. How's your sink doing?" Realizing immediately the stupidity of his question.

"It's doing fine...thank you."

"My best friend's daughter is playing. I come to as many of her games as I can."

"How nice. I'm sure she appreciates that, Mr. Dunning."

"Please call me Richard." At that moment the buzzer sounded again calling all the players back to the floor.

"Aah, I guess you have to get back to the game."

"Yes, I do." She said sitting her bottle of water down.

Richard watched as she walked back on the floor and blew her whistle to begin the game. He made his way back to his seat thinking he had never sounded so stupid talking to a woman before in his entire life.

"Dude, where's the hot dogs?" Adam asked. "I thought you were going after hot dogs?"

"Oh, yeah, sorry, man. I'll be right back."

During the second half, the crowd was going nuts. They were now into overtime with the score tied at forty-six. It was either team's game. The girls looked sweaty and tired. The other referee appeared to be ready to have this game finished too, but Caroline looked as fresh and beautiful as she had every time he had seen her, even in black and white stripes.

Richard's plan was to catch her again after the game and if the opportunity presented itself he would ask if he could call her sometime. The buzzer blew loudly bringing Richard out of his musings. The game was over and the Cougars were on their way to the championship. The excited fans flooded the court congratulating the players, but Richard had much more important matters to attend to. He watched to see which way Caroline was headed. Giving the excuse he saw someone he knew and wanted to say hello, not a complete untruth. He told Adam he would look for him on the floor before leaving,

Where did she go? She's gone. Slightly panicked, he didn't see her anywhere. Richard stood close to the scorer's table with his hands on his hips looking toward the exits and the crowd, but there was no referee in sight. As many games as he had attended, he never had paid any attention to when the refs left after a game, but they obviously left immediately.

Finding Adam and his family, Richard waited with them for Lindsey to come out of the locker room before going home.

"Great game, kid." Adam rubbed Lindsey's head and gave her a hug. Everyone in her family congratulated her for playing a good game and making it to the championship. Richard asked about the date and location of the next game and quickly wondered if Caroline would be officiating that game as well.

"Will you have the same refs or will there be a different set to call that game?" The question sounded ridiculous even to his ears, but he had to know. He was sure no one suspected a thing.

"You never know," Adam replied.

"Anyone up for some ice cream?" Richard asked, trying to redirect the conversation before his motives were discovered. The kids were definitely up for it.

Basketball season was complete for Caroline, and in a way she was glad. The extra money sure came in handy, but she was ready for a break. But suddenly she remembered Richard coming up to her at one of the games. It was odd to her then and still is now. Thinking, doesn't he know the fans don't come up and talk to the refs? She also recalled their conversation while he was repairing her sink, 'Have we met somewhere before?' Shaking her head, what a line, she thought. To her, it seemed odd that Richard appeared confident when talking to her in her home, but at the game he seemed to be a bit of a goober.

After the passing of her husband, Caroline's mother advised her to be very careful and not give men the wrong idea. "It doesn't take much for them to get the wrong one." She had taken her mother's advice. She was very aware during conversations, even casual ones, with men she didn't know well. The notion replayed in her head causing her to wonder if Mr. Dunning was seeking her attention. The thought caused her to feel a bit uneasy.

❧ CHAPTER EIGHT ❧

Schools in the middle Tennessee area were out for summer break. Joshua had a summer job at a local pizza restaurant that kept him busy. He loved the employee discount and used it often. Caroline had planned a five day vacation the following week in beautiful Gatlinburg for her and her son. Her brother offered her the use of his timeshare at the Westgate Smoky Mountain Resort & Spa since they were unable to use their week this year. She was looking forward to spending a week up in the mountains, as was Joshua. He had saved some money of his own and planned to have as much fun as his wallet would allow.

"Caroline…sweetie, what's the hold up?" Melissa asked from the living room.

"She's a female, Aunt Melissa. You women take forever to get ready to go someplace. I used to think it was just my mom, but then Papaw told me Mamaw takes forever too. And my friends tell me that it takes their sisters hours to get ready to go anywhere. Eric told me his sister gets up at five o'clock every morning to get ready to leave for school by seven-thirty. Now, tell me what guy do you know that takes that long to get dressed for any occasion?"

Melissa grinned at Joshua. "Oh yeah, well, you wouldn't believe what we women go through just to look beautiful for you men," she teased back.

"Finally! Now can we go?" Melissa said when Caroline walked into the room.

"I can't believe I let you talk me into this. Joshua, honey, I won't be out late. And I have my cell phone, so call if you need to."

"Mooom. I'll be fine."

Melissa and Caroline arrived at the Hunters Lane High School for their reunion within twenty minutes of leaving the house. Caroline was sort of dreading it, but told herself to just enjoy the evening and let Melissa have her fun. They had already gone through the yearbook to refresh their memories of faces and names, they would talk about who looked the worst and had aged the most for days to come.

Caroline and Melissa stopped at the table just inside the door to pick up their name tags. The lady coordinating the table was none other than Janice Mayhew Tensely, the woman responsible for this shindig. During High School, Janice preferred to do all the work herself with planning such things without letting others getting involved, but tonight it appeared she had a few volunteers helping her.

Always a beauty, Janice had aged well, just a slightly older version of the girl they remembered. Her popularity and school spirit made her an excellent cheerleader. Throughout high school, she possessed blemish free skin and salon perfect hair every day. Her long, painted nails completed the picture.

The girl seemed to have it all, all but just one thing. A passing grade in math. This almost caused her to be put on academic probation with Cheerleading. Math took a toll on her. This is where Melissa saw an opportunity and swooped down on it. She was a wiz at math, and even though Janice was a year ahead it still was fairly easy for Melissa. In the tenth grade, Melissa had a crush on Jonathan Brown, who was good friends with Janice. The two gals worked out at deal where Melissa would help Janice with her math if Janice would introduce her to Jonathan. By mid-term the plan seemed to be working. Janice made a B in math, and Melissa went to the homecoming game with Jonathan. Melissa was curious if Janice remembered all the drama from that one semester. She by now had forgotten about it until she and Caroline were going through the yearbook.

Within fifteen minutes, Caroline and Melissa received their name tags along with a cold soft drink and began to mingle in the gymnasium. Not long after that, Adam and his lovely wife Sabrina arrived and began the same process. Soft music played in the background as the crowd grew. A dull roar of voices hovered in the rafters.

Former classmates milled around the gym. It was funny to hear many people introduce themselves to someone they saw daily for several years a long time ago.

"Melissa?"

"Yes?" she responded turning to see who was speaking her name.

"Hi. Remember me? Jonathan Brown."

"Jonathan, oh my, yes, I do remember you. How are you?" Melissa would not have recognized him if he had not introduced himself and had pinned a small printout of his senior picture on his shirt. The man had gained fifty pounds and lost fifty percent of his hair. But when he smiled, she could see a hint of the young man she had a crush on all those years ago. Her reaction to him made her wonder what he thought of her being twenty years older.

As Melissa was catching up with Jonathan, Carmen joined the little group and began a conversation with Caroline. Carmen sat with Caroline and Melissa at the lunch table every day. She informed and updated everyone of the dating scene and who went to detention. She was currently working as a newspaper reporter.

"Do you think he will show?" Sabrina asked noticing her husband continually look around the room.

"Probably not. When I reminded him, he just said he doubted it." Just then Sabrina saw the subject of their conversation step inside.

"Dude, I didn't think you were going to show." Adam said to Richard as he walked up to him and Sabrina sticking his name tag on.

"Yeah, well…I didn't have anything better to do this evening. Adam, do you remember all these people?" Richard said looking around the gym seeing many unfamiliar faces.

"No. Not all of them, but a lot of these people still live in the Nashville area, and I see them from time to time in different places. Some are our neighbors and a few of them go to our church. You, Richard, have been gone too long, and are out of touch."

"Yeah, well…not with my real friends." He said slapping Adam on the back. "I'm going to grab something to drink. I'll be right back." For someone who didn't think he knew anyone other than Adam and Sabrina, he had no trouble talking with two guys he had biology with while waiting in line for his Coca-Cola.

"Oh look, Sabrina is here," Caroline said to Melissa. "Let's go over."

"Hi, Sabrina, Adam. I didn't know you two were coming."

"Caroline, hi. I didn't know you were coming either. Hi, Melissa. It's good to see you again."

"And it's good to see you too, Sabrina, Adam. See many people you know?"

"Well, some. It was Adam that graduated from Hunters Lane, but I am seeing a lot of people we both know from high school, college and currently. This is a really good turn out."

Reconnecting, the small group was laughing in between their chatter when Richard noticed Caroline from across the gym. His jaw dropped open as if he had just seen the most amazing thing.

Thinking to himself, Caroline? Is that Caroline Martin over there talking to my best friend? Suddenly happy about his decision to attend this social event, Richard quickened his pace back to Adam and Sabrina.

"Hey Richard, this is Caroline…"

"Caroline Martin. Yes we've met on a couple of occasions," Richard said cutting Adam off.

"Alright, but do you know her friend Melissa?" Adam asked continuing the introductions. Suddenly remembering Richard had asked about Caroline at one of Lindsey's ballgames caused him to stifle a grin.

"No, I'm sorry, I don't." Adam continued and explained how he and his wife knew these two ladies. "We attend the same church as Caroline. And Melissa and I work at the same office. By the way, Melissa, where is Alex?"

"I couldn't get him to come. He hates these things. He won't even go to his family reunion, much less one from his high school."

The five seemed to have plenty to talk about until a former classmate interrupted Richard. There were many people there that remembered Richard, and with a little help, he remembered them. While the gym echoed with conversations, the announcement for the buffet was clearly heard.

Caroline didn't admit to meeting Richard before tonight, nor did she act as if they knew each other now.

Richard grabbed Adam's arm and spoke in a low voice where only he could hear. The women had begun moving towards the large, round, beautifully decorated tables to set their drinks down to save themselves a seat.

"Why didn't you tell me you knew Caroline and that you went to church with her?"

"I go to church with a lot of people. Do you want me to tell you all their names?" Adam teased. "What's the matter with you?" he asked laughing knowing very well what the situation was with Richard.

Letting go of his friend's arm, Richard walked faster to get closer to Caroline in the buffet line with hopes of sitting next to her at the table.

"Oh, this is going to be a fun evening," Adam whispered in his wife's ear.

MOOSH Catering provided the dinner. Richard was so busy with Caroline he barely tasted the food. Eating was the last thing on his mind this evening. Adam, however, had seconds as he watched with much enjoyment his best buddy work at getting a woman's attention. He had to prevent himself from laughing out loud. He had never seen Richard work this hard at anything.

"This is a great turn out isn't it?" Melissa commented as she looked around the room at the people after she and Caroline sat down at the table.

"Sure is. I would have never thought there would be this many here," Caroline responded looking around at the crowd.

"So, Caroline, what year did you graduate? If you don't mind me asking. I mean, I'm sure you are several years behind me and Adam," Richard asked.

Ha-ha- good save Rich, old man. Good save, Adam thought as he ate his chicken.

"Class of '93. Melissa and I both. We were best friends all through school and still are." Caroline responded smiling at her friend while silently pleading for help from this man who kept talking to her. Melissa either didn't get the hint or was letting her friend fend for herself.

Richard didn't repulse Caroline. She thought he was very nice looking. She simply feared he would mistake her kindness for flirting or being interested.

"That's funny. It appears you and Adam are best friends from school like Caroline and me," Melissa added.

"Yes, very funny," Adam answered for his friend.

"That was a delicious meal. Didn't you think so, Adam?" Sabrina asked her husband.

"Yes, it was. I wonder what's for dessert. I hope it's as good as the main course."

Moosh Catering featured homemade pies and cakes that were rated second to none. They prided themselves on cooking and baking from scratch.

Adam returned carrying two small plates with a large slice of coconut cake and a small piece of chocolate pie for his wife.

"I think I'm going to have the pie, what about you, Melissa? Come, let's get our dessert."

Melissa followed Caroline as suggested. However, she could not pass up the opportunity to ask questions.

"So, have you met Richard before? And if that answer is yes, you have some explaining to do as to why you haven't told me about it."

"He repaired my bathroom sink several weeks ago, that's all. And he showed up at one of the ballgames I worked. When he sees me, he wants to talk to me. I don't do one thing to encourage him."

"He seems pretty nice and he's an old friend of Adam's. If there were a problem, he would surely tell you."

"Yes. You're right. Adam or Sabrina would tell me." Relieved by Melissa's comment, Caroline felt a little more relaxed when she returned to the table.

"You know what would be perfect with this cake, honey? A tall glass of ice cold milk."

"I doubt they have milk. After all, we're big kids now. We can drink coffee with our dessert," she giggled. Adam reached over and gave his wife a quick kiss. He loved the way she teased him.

Richard took advantage of the ladies being in the dessert line to began his inquiry.

"Ok, let's have it. How long have the two of you known Caroline?"

"We've known her for years. Like I said we attend the same church, and her son is in the youth group Sabrina and I work with. You interested?" Richard opened his mouth to reply when the two ladies rejoined the group at the table, but quickly closed it.

Richard noticed that Caroline was less distant to him as she appeared the other times he had attempted to talk to her. This caused him to relax just slightly enough to ask a big question.

The buffet tables were cleared allowing for the dance floor. Couples headed out as the music started to play.

"Come on, Sabrina. Dance with me, woman," Adam said as he stood taking his wife's hand.

"How can I resist? After all they are playing our song." The comment was an inside joke. The song playing was not theirs at all.

Many couples moved to the music. Melissa danced with several partners. Each guy she knew well enough to know it would not be misunderstood and was just casual. In the meantime, Richard and Caroline found themselves alone at the table.

Caroline wanted to bolt, but remained glued to her chair. She needed her best friend beside her, but knew that was ridiculous. She was no longer a teenager, but a grown woman. Richard was waiting for the right moment. And finally a slow song sounded through the speakers and he asked.

"Would you care to dance? I promise I won't step on your toes."

Quick, run! Caroline's mind screamed. "Aahh…Nooo, I don't think…"

Standing and extending his hand he gently coaxed her. "Come on. It'll be fun."

Many years had passed since Caroline shared a dance with a man. Convinced that this would be a total disaster, she actually found herself in confident hands. Growing up, Richard's mother made him and his siblings take dance lessons which of course he and his brother hated. However, in high school, he appreciated it. But never more than he did at this moment.

Richard held Caroline neither too closely nor too tightly. He couldn't believe it; his heart raced as he slowly guided the most beautiful woman he had ever seen around the dance floor.

"You dance very well," Caroline commented. She too amazed by herself that she had not forgotten how to dance.

"Thank you. So do you."

Unfortunately, the waltz being played quickly caused Craig to come to Caroline's mind. It usually made her a little sad. She attempted to distract her thoughts of him and the way he used to hold her closely, his hand firmly against her lower back when they danced. Richard's hand sat higher than where Craig's would have been. Thankfully, Richard spoke and drew her out of her musings. When the song ended, the D.J. announced a fun country line dance. Most joined in and enjoyed the camaraderie with huge smiles and laughter.

Richard and Caroline walked toward the table after the line dance finished, but Adam and Sabrina hurried him back on the floor for the Electric Slide. Caroline took advantage to sit this one out and encouraged Richard to go ahead. Richard could do the Electric Slide like no one else, and Adam refused to let his friend sit on the sidelines. Caroline declined, but insisted, "No, please, go ahead."

Sitting, Caroline gazed at this man boldly having fun out on the dance floor oblivious to those around him. The man could dance. It was obvious to everyone including her. By this time Melissa had joined her sipping a cold drink while she rested and cooled off. Melissa noticed her friend watching the people out on the dance floor. Quick to conclude, she was looking at someone in particular.

"I think someone is having a good time."

"Yes, I do believe you are," Caroline teased causing Melissa to laugh out loud.

Richard didn't want the night to come to an end. It was possibly the best night of his life. He would be sure to thank Adam for reminding him about the event later. But for now, the hour was late and people were starting to leave, he didn't want to pass up this chance to ask Caroline if he could call her sometime.

"Melissa, I guess we should be going. It's later than I thought, and I told Joshua I wouldn't be out too late."

Melissa looked at her watch. "Eleven o'clock! Whoa, I had no idea it was this late."

"You girls afraid you'll turn into pumpkins by midnight?" Adam teased.

"Yeah, and our carriage will turn back into mice," Caroline responded causing everyone around them to laugh.

Richard's heart raced rapidly. It was now or never. He spoke where only Caroline could hear him.

"You know, I almost didn't come to this thing…but I'm glad I did. I had a wonderful time. Caroline, I would like to call you sometime… if you don't mind that is."

"Aahh, well, I…that may be all right." She silently scolded herself, Aaah!…why did I say that? Now he will probably call tomorrow! She had no idea why she answered the way she did, but Caroline made Richard one happy man with her response.

Melissa reached for her purse as did Caroline.

"May I walk you ladies out to your car?" Richard asked.

"Oh no, thank you. We can manage. Good night everyone," Melissa answered.

"See you Sunday, Caroline," Sabrina said as the two ladies got up from their chairs.

An idea instantly sprang into Richard's head. Sunday, that's right. Caroline goes to the same church as Adam and Sabrina. I may have to start going to church again.

Looking at her watch, Sabrina spoke. "Come on Adam, the party's over, dear. It's time to go home."

"Yeah, I guess so. Well Rich, I'm thinking you're glad you came to this lame event after all," he said jokingly.

Staring at his friend with an odd expression, he responded. "I cannot believe this. I see this gorgeous woman at a hardware store, and she gives me the brush-off. Then I find myself in her home for a repair job, and again the brush-off. Then I go to a basketball game and there she is officiating the game. When I approach her, she barely speaks to me. I keep going to ballgames just so I can see her, and hopefully talk to her. But no, she's not there. Then I get badgered by you to come to a school reunion that I really do not want to attend, but I do for who knows why, and there you two stand talking to the very woman I have been trying to find, talk to, and get to know. Then if that was not enough, I find out you two go to church with this woman…and have for years. Adam, I don't know which I want to do most right now, hug you or punch you in the face."

Adam and Sabrina laughed at their friend as they rose from the table to leave.

"Oh, by the way, what time does church start?" Richard asked as he sat slumped in his chair with his hands in his pockets.

"Worship service begins at eleven," Adam answered over his shoulder as he put his arm around his wife's waist and made their way toward the exit.

Melissa pulled out of the parking lot and onto the highway barely able to contain herself.

"It looked as if you and Richard were having a nice time talking…and dancing."

"I did have a good time. I'm glad I came after all. Richard turned out to be a pretty nice guy."

"So he came to fix your sink. How did that go?"

"Well, let's see...he fixed the sink. Gave me the bill. I paid him, and then he left. What's the matter with you?"

"So, what did you learn about him? Is he someone you would want to get to know better?"

"You're not going to let this go are you?" Caroline said with a bit of a chuckle.

"As we both learned this evening, he is Adam's friend and former classmate that I have run into a few times. He came and fixed my sink several weeks ago, and then he pops up at a few ballgames that I worked. And that my dear friend, is all there is."

"All there is? No ma'am. I do not believe that's all there is. The man could not take his eyes off of you the whole evening. You two danced several dances together, which I was happy to see you do, but I don't think that is the end. I think I will be hearing about this man in the near future."

"Melissa, you've lost it. There is nothing, and there will be nothing. We just had a fun evening at a school reunion. That's all. And by the way, do you remember him from school?"

"No, can't say that I do, but it was a big school. And he was a year ahead of us. We didn't know Adam then either."

Pulling into the drive brought their evening to a close. "Well, here you are. Thanks for going with me. I know you really didn't want to go, and I'm thankful you did. Besides, girlfriend, you had a good time."

"Good night, Melissa," Caroline said in a sing-song voice as she got out of the car.

❧ CHAPTER NINE ❦

It was one in the morning and Richard's mind buzzed with thoughts of Caroline. He hated nights like this, but this night the subject of his insomnia not only kept him awake, but also frustrated him. Unable to find her when he actively sought her out, but when he stopped, she appeared. Her fickleness baffled him. Attempting to talk to her resulted in no feedback. A few weeks later they sat next to each other talking while at the class reunion he wasn't planning to attend. Now the next hurdle was timing his phone call. His first thought was to call her as soon as he returned home that night, but the small part of his brain that was actually functioning correctly told him that would be a bad idea. Maybe he would wait a day or two, let her know who was in charge. Which begged the question: who was in charge and of what? He decided to call tomorrow afternoon.

Two forty-seven was the last number Richard saw on his clock radio, sleep finally winning out. This particular Saturday he was not due to be in the office until ten o'clock, so he could sleep in a little which he did without remorse.

Todd sat at the desk talking on the phone when Richard arrived looking a little rough around the edges. Sidney prepared her schedule for the day. Although it took extra time, she was content waiting for a chance to see Richard. She always tried to greet the boss before starting her day, Sidney knew Richard's schedule almost as well as he did. She usually made coffee if needed and had a cup on his desk when he walked in.

"Sidney. Why are you here? You're off today," Richard said with a hint of confusion.

"Yes, well, not today. Rob called in with a stomach bug or something, so I'm covering for him. Forgive me for asking, but do you feel alright?"

"Yes. Why?"

"You look like you either don't feel well, or you're tired."

"Tired. I was up pretty late last night."

Todd hung up the phone and began speaking to Richard as he gave her some work instructions.

"So, how was the party?" Todd asked.

Sidney wondered what party, but didn't ask. With her list in hand, she left the office. She wished she could hear more party details, but she was being paid to work, not socialize.

"It was great. Funny thing was I was expecting it to be a big bore, but there's this lady I've seen around town lately. And she was there and gave life to the whole evening."

Todd didn't contain his chuckle, "Yeah, they'll do that from time to time."

Todd worked until two. Richard stayed until four. He figured Brian would be in the office next week and would want things to be in order. Truthfully it was Richard who wanted things in order. The system he held to was a place for everything and everything in its place. In college, he and his roommate lived like slobs and didn't care. His first apartment appeared much the same way. One day he was looking for a bowl for his breakfast cereal only to find there wasn't a single dish, pan or utensil clean. The sink was filled with dirty dishes, and the counter was a collection of empty cereal boxes, cans and trash that he was too lazy to throw out. Disgusted by his own mess, he spent two hours cleaning just the kitchen. He then tackled the entire apartment that was equally as cluttered and dirty. That day he realized he disliked living this way and despised even more wasting so much of his time doing such mindless work. Suddenly, while picking up his dirty laundry a brilliant idea came to his mind. Each day if I don't throw anything on the floor I won't have anything to pick up. And if I put a dish in the dishwasher when I'm finished using it, it will be getting loaded without me having to actually load it. Only problem is I will still need to unload the dishes after they are cleaned, and I'll have to actually put the clothes away after washing them. As Richard unloaded the sink, he decided he would give his idea a serious try. He did not want to spend that kind of time cleaning anything ever again. So, from that day forward he kept his home and office neat and orderly with everything placed where it belonged.

Nervously tapping in Caroline's phone number, Richard took a deep breath letting it out slowly as he waited for her to answer. Prepared and alone in the office with a large Coca-Cola on ice sitting within reach he anticipated the sound of her voice. The phone rang several times, and Richard was starting to fear Caroline was not available when she finally answered.

"Hello." Her voice was soft and sounded lovely to his ears. He could listen to that voice forever.

"Hi, Caroline, this is Richard. I hope I haven't called at a bad time."

Caroline wasn't surprised to hear his voice. She feared he would call this soon and actually wished he had forgotten. She really had no interest in leading him on or getting something started that she knew would not end well. She considered what to do.

"Hi, aahhh, no, no it's not a bad time."

"Good, I'm actually at the office. I've just finished my work and it's quiet here so I can talk in peace." A few seconds of awkward silence followed.

"So tell me, how long have you known Adam and Sabrina?" He already knew the answer to that question, but he needed something safe to say, something to get a conversation going. He had considered many topics to chat to her about, but all had abandoned him, and now he sat there with nothing.

"We've gone to the same church for quite a few years. I know his wife mostly. They are lovely people. Adam also works with the teens, so my son Joshua knows Adam pretty well...He's great with the kids."

"Yeah, that's because inside he's still a kid himself," Richard teased causing Caroline to chuckle at his banter, which relieved him instantly.

Something shifted in Caroline. For reasons unknown, she felt the need to ask this man personal questions. At the same time her head was screaming at her to hang up the phone and not allow this to go any farther. She continued in conversation.

"How long have you lived in this area, Richard?"

"Several weeks…and all my life." Richard took the time to explain to Caroline that he was born and raised here. After college he had moved away from the area until his brother's recent accident.

"So, you're not a plumber by trade?"

"Yes, and no."

"You seem to have both ends of the answer to everything, don't you?" she teased.

"It would appear that way," he chuckled. "Dunning Plumbing was started by my dad, but he is now retired and my brother, Brian, runs it. I'm just helping out until he gets back on his feet. I live in Atlanta and did work at a pharmaceutical company, and not to blow my own horn, but I was one of the top reps in that company. Then my boss interfered with my clients, which interfered with my pay, so I quit my job. All this happened at the same time Brian had his accident. And since I have no wife or kids to keep me in Atlanta, it freed me up to come help my brother."

"Wow. Is Brian your only sibling?"

"No, I have an older sister, Katie. She lives here in Goodlettsville with her husband and kids. I'm in the middle."

"You know what they say about the middle child," she playfully taunted again. The fact that Caroline felt comfortable talking to this man and kept teasing him was surprising to her.

"Ha-haaa, yes I do." There was a brief moment of silence before he continued. "So what about you? Where do you spend your days?"

"I work at Vanderbilt University Medical Center. I'm not a nurse or doctor. But if you get hurt or sick, depending on how bad you are, and are brought to Vanderbilt, you may find yourself at my desk answering a few questions before being seen by one of our doctors."

"You mean like the emergency room part of Vanderbilt?"

"Yes, the ER. Monday through Friday I'm there…and on an occasional weekend. But mostly I'm daytime during the week."

"Is Joshua your only child?"

"Yes, he is my only one."

Cautiously, Richard asked another question that he felt necessary. "Would it be too personal if I ask what happened to Joshua's father?"

"No. When Joshua was two years old, his father was killed. He was a sergeant in the Marines leading his squad in convoy security for humanitarian aid when his squad was ambushed. He was wounded after his HUMVEE was hit with a rocket-propelled grenade. Even though he was severely wounded, he was able to drag two other injured Marines to safety. He was a hero."

"Oh, I'm sorry to hear that." Truly saddened that Joshua didn't have a father, Richard on the other hand wasn't sorry that Caroline didn't have an ex-husband somewhere to deal with.

Richard sat with his feet propped on the desk as he leaned back in his chair. He turned slightly to his left when he noticed outside the sun was going down. The conversation had gone on for two hours. To Richard, it seemed only a few minutes.

"I cannot believe we have been talking for two hours. I hope I haven't kept you from anything important. Truth is I've enjoyed our conversation very much."

"Oh, has it been that long? I really need to get off the phone and get supper started," she said with a hint of laughter in her voice.

"Yeah, I should too...not get supper started," he teased, "But get a little more work done before I call it a day. I hope to talk to you again...real soon." She returned her good bye and he touched the end call button on his phone.

Looking around the office he wondered what to do next. Distracted he failed to come up with anything. Well, that's it...I'm totally useless for the rest of the day, he concluded.

Caroline hurried to the kitchen to find something to prepare quickly for supper. Joshua would be home in a half hour. She threw some spaghetti in a pot and turned the burner on high. Immediately scolding herself out loud, "Oh that's great, spaghetti for someone who has worked around Italian food all day...real good, Caroline, real good." It was too late to change the menu the spaghetti was already in the water.

After putting the meatballs in the oven, she quickly called Melissa. She had to talk to her immediately.

Melissa was in the middle of cooking supper as well, but listened to her recount her previous two hours. Caroline was talking so fast she could do nothing but listen.

"I figured he would call me, Melissa. Now he will probably call again. What am I to do?"

"What? Slow down. Who called?"

"Richard Dunning, the guy we met at the school reunion."

"Oh, that guy. Is it bad that he called you?"

"Yes. No...I don't know. Melissa, it has been a lot of years since I talked that long to a guy over the phone...or anywhere for that matter."

"Oh, so it was a long conversation?" Melissa said smiling to herself.

"Melissa, I can tell you are smiling. This isn't funny. I just don't know what to do about this."

"What's the problem? Did you not enjoy talking with him? Do you not want him to call?"

Caroline couldn't remember that last time she spent two hours on the phone with a man she just met and enjoyed it. She had been alone many years and figured an innocent conversation with him would be harmless.

"I enjoyed talking to him more than I thought I would, but I just don't know. I mean..." A few silent seconds passed when Caroline confessed her fears. "What will Joshua say? What if this guy turns out to be a jerk? I don't know if I really want to go down this path, Melissa. I have done fine without a man in my life since Craig, well, with the exception of my son. I don't know if I want to shake things up. Relationships can be one big pain at times."

"Yes, they can, but so can being alone. Caroline, you will never have a relationship with anyone on any level that is perfect because people are not perfect. Even our relationship as best friends isn't perfect. It has been just you and Joshua for a long time because that is the way you have wanted it, and there isn't anything wrong with that. But, Caroline, sweetie, I see how men look at you. You are a very attractive, desirable woman. And there is a man out there somewhere that will love you and treat you right like Craig did, but it will be different because it won't be Craig. I'm not saying Richard is that man, but who knows."

Caroline and Melissa spoke until Joshua pulled into the driveway. Melissa recognized her friend feared the unknown. Her concerns centered around ending up with a man that would eventually break her heart, or worse, mistreat her or Joshua. Up to this moment Caroline wasn't willing to take that chance.

"Sweetie, I really think it will be alright. Adam knows this guy. And if you're not sure maybe, you should talk to him and Sabrina and just ask them point blank what kind of man Richard Dunning is. And if you decide you may want to get to know him a little better, just take it very slow and tell him it's slow or it's no."

Later that night, Caroline lay in bed reading a book, or trying to, but her mind kept replaying her conversation with Melissa. She had read the same paragraph three times and still didn't know what it said. She trusted her friend to help clear her head and to give her solid advice. Just go slow she reminded herself. Closing her book she laid it on the side table and turned the TV on instead. She watched an old movie with Audrey Hepburn until she drifted off to sleep.

Sunday morning, Richard prepared to do something he hadn't done in many years, and finding it a little hard to believe while in the process. Heads would turn, eyebrows would rise, and explanations would be in order, but he was going to do it. He was attending church.

Pacing back and forth in the kitchen drinking his third cup of coffee, he looked at his watch again. Only five minutes had passed since the last time he looked.

"I cannot believe I am about to do this," he said to himself out loud while pacing and drinking his coffee. In his professional life, Richard prioritized working hard. He managed his time well and sacrificed many Saturdays for his career. But on Sundays the man drew the line. Sunday was the day of rest and the good Lord Himself had said so. Richard obeyed this rule consistently, which for him meant relaxation and ballgames.

As a given on these days, Richard usually slept in until at least seven-thirty. While in Atlanta, his habit was to shower, dress and stop by The Coffee Beanery. His order and routine never varied from a large cappuccino and a banana nut muffin while he read the newspaper. In Goodlettsville, this remained the same except he subbed at Krispy Kreme doughnuts. Around ten-thirty or so, he would head back to his sister's house where he did some laundry and watched TV while the family attended church services. At midday he drove to his parents' to watch the game with his dad, who enjoyed sports as much as he did. To Richard, the perfect Sunday consisted of an entire day of sports. Am I actually going to spend two hours or longer listening to a man in a suit and tie judge me and tell me what 'Thou Shalt Not Do'? And all just to be near the woman that has invaded my mind, He thought to himself. This was definitely not Richard's idea of worshiping the Lord. He had sweet memories of attending church while growing up. Voices singing hymns and a loving pastor teaching you about the Lord and how to live a

Christian life. But several years ago something happened to Richard that destroyed that part of his life.

"Alright. If you're going to do it, it's time you left," he said again to himself. It was a good thing the family had already left for church, or they would have thought he had gone crazy.

Richard pulled out of the driveway and headed for the Marydale Bible Church where his best friend and the woman he so wanted to get to know attended weekly.

❧ CHAPTER TEN ❧

Adam could not believe his eyes when he saw Richard Dunning walking through the church doors. It had to be a solid ten years since Richard stepped voluntarily inside one without it being a wedding or a funeral.

"Hi, Rich. Glad you could make it today. What's the occasion, or should I say who?" Adam said knowing fully his motives. He and Richard hopped on every opportunity to razz each other about everything. Teasing his friend about coming to church to possibly see a woman was fair game. Richard would do the same to him in a heartbeat, but much worse.

"Funny, Adam. Is that the best you got? I can't believe I let you hang out with me all these years."

At that time the pastor came toward them with a smile and extending his hand to kindly greet Adam and Richard.

"Hello, Brother Whitehurst, this is …"

"Todd Dunning's son, right?"

"Yes, Sir. And you are one of his buddies, aren't you?" The two men shared a hearty hand-shake. Richard had forgotten about his dad's good friend being a preacher.

"Yes, me and Todd go back a long way. As a matter of fact, he and I had lunch a few days ago. He told me one of his sons was back in town to help out the other. I just didn't know which one. I never could keep you boys apart."

After a brief conversation, it was time for the service to begin. The two moved inside and sat with the rest of Adam's family. Settled into his seat, he looked for Caroline, but could not find her.

The service began with one of the elderly men of the congregation walking up to the podium to open the service with a word of prayer. His face was weathered and his hair white, but when this man prayed, it appeared he was speaking face to face with God. Richard felt like he was intruding on a private conversation.

If Richard were asked to define the song service in one word, he would say powerful. All around the room people sang from a hymnbook accompanied by a piano, organ, and of course a guitar; after all, this was the Music City. Another man stepped behind the podium to make a few announcements, and as he did so Richard took the opportunity to discreetly scan the room for Caroline, the reason for his attendance.

The choir rose and began singing with joy and vigor from their hearts. The song was vaguely familiar. He thought he may have heard it a few times while growing up, but wasn't certain. It definitely was not one heard on local Christian radio stations. The lyrics were about a meeting in the air and how all of heaven will be there. Richard found himself in awe of what he heard. The voices were a blend of young, middle-aged and seniors that lingered in a person's mind after the music finished. He definitely could not remember hearing such beauty before.

The pastor began his sermon and Richard was becoming agitated because he was unable find Caroline. Then it dawned on him that she was probably sitting behind him. He certainly couldn't turn around and look. That would just be rude. But he could slightly adjust his angle to broaden his view.

Brother Whitehurst, the pastor, was an older man like his dad, but his age had no negative effect on his preaching. He spoke for about forty minutes without repeating himself. He hit the important words hard and they were noticed. Even though Richard's mind was centered on Caroline, he did catch a few of those important words. But there was something he said that would stick in Richard's head for days to come.

"At one time or another in all of our lives we have forgotten about God, but He has never for one second forgotten about YOU or me. Let's pray together as we close the service."

After church, Adam invited Richard to lunch with him and his family and he happily accepted. Adam noticed how Richard's eyes kept wandering around the large auditorium as they talked. It was hard to not laugh at his friend, but witnessing Richard's world being turned upside down over a pretty face was definitely comical.

Someone called Adam away and Richard seized a few moments alone with Sabrina.

"Sabrina, I don't see Caroline anywhere, or Melissa. I thought they came to this church."

"Caroline does, but I haven't seen her today. She is usually here every week," she replied letting her eyes scan across the room. "Maybe she's working in the nursery."

Unlike her husband Sabrina wasn't going to tease Richard. She could see the disappointment in his eyes that Caroline was not in attendance.

Not knowing exactly how to handle his next move, Richard fought the urge to call Caroline again when he returned home from church. He considered this logically, its been less than twenty- four hours since I called, maybe I should wait until tomorrow. Don't want to scare her off, he reasoned.

⚭

It was a rough start on Monday. Richard overslept which he rarely ever did, then spilled coffee down his shirt forcing him to change, which added to his tardiness. Once he did get to work, things were just not going well. Sidney noticed and made an effort to make his day better.

"Here, Richard. You just sit down, and I'll get you a cup of coffee."

"Thanks, Sidney, but…" She was already at the coffee pot outside his office filling a cup just the way he liked it. She also brought him a cream-filled Krispy Kreme doughnut from the box one of the other guys had brought in this morning.

"Thank you. I didn't know you knew how I drank my coffee," he commented after taking a sip.

"Just something I've noticed," she responded. While Sidney was in Richard's office the two of them went over some paperwork for a few past jobs. Sidney really enjoyed the feel of the office. She wondered if she would be suited for working behind a desk, answering the phones and such. But then she remembered it was the pay that had her working such a job in the first place. She often speculated about how Richard saw her. Did he see her as just an employee or a friend? This was followed by another curious thought that had plagued her at other times. Did Richard even see her as a woman? She quickly stopped her musing when Katie came in looking all feminine and pretty and handed her a work order.

"Sidney, I love that perfume you're wearing," Katie commented.

"Thank you. You don't think it's too much do you?"

"Oh no. It is just a hint and it's lovely."

Sidney had never worn perfume to work before. She hoped Katie was not the only one who noticed.

Oversleeping wasn't the culprit that caused Richard's day to be off. The expectation of seeing Caroline on Sunday and it not happening was to blame. Richard had never put so much energy into pursuing a woman, and certainly never attended church just to see her. As he sat logging in on his computer he felt as if he had lost control of his life and he did not like the feeling. Focusing on the days' agenda was sure to keep Caroline from invading his thoughts.

Richard finished supper with Katie and her family. Even though his life was not going as he wanted, Katie kept his stomach happy. It was a beautiful summer night in middle Tennessee. Richard couldn't decide which to do, sit out on the back porch with Katie and Russ and put Caroline out of his mind, or call her. Seeing his sister and her husband sitting together on the swing enjoying a glass of iced-tea Richard felt an ache inside he could no longer ignore. He chose to call Caroline.

"Hello."

"Hi Caroline. It's Richard." He decided against telling her about going to church yesterday. He didn't want to feel any more foolish than he already did. "Is this a bad time to call?"

"No, not at all. It's beautiful here in Gatlinburg."

"Gatlinburg?" So much for not feeling foolish…again… Richard took a deep breath.

"Yes, Joshua and I are vacationing in The Smokey Mountains this week. We arrived yesterday afternoon."

"Oh, I'm sorry. I didn't know. I guess you are busy doing something fun, and I should let you go do that." Immediately Richard berated himself, *Can you not speak to this woman without sounding like a big idiot?*

"No, it's fine. We just finished eating supper and are waiting for the check. We're at the Best Italian Café Pizzeria. You would think Joshua would be tired of pizza, but not so. It's his favorite place to eat in Gatlinburg."

"Well, we all have our faves."

Richard didn't keep Caroline on the line too long not wanting to interrupt their vacation. After he closed up his phone, he wondered why she hadn't mentioned going to Gatlinburg the other day during their long conversation. Richard's self doubt came smacking him right in the face like a fist out of nowhere in a comic strip.

Sitting at his desk as if he had all the free time in the world, Richard slowly drank his coffee. His usual motivation halted and his spirits low, he confronted an oddity. He had never experienced such a case of the blahs as today. Someone knocked on the door and roused him a bit.

"It's open. Oh hi, Sid. What can I do for ya?" He asked his disinterest obvious.

"Nothing. Just have a later appointment, so I'm killing time. Thought I would stick my head in and say hello." It was common for some of the employees to stop in Richard's office for a few minutes to chat if they had the time, and Richard didn't look too busy.

"You look like you lost your best friend."

"No, it's nothing like that."

"I have an appointment way out in Brentwood, so you probably won't see me again today. Wanted to make sure you didn't think I was somewhere slacking off."

"I wouldn't think that, Sid. You're one I can always rely on." Richard missed the look on her face. His words pierced right through to her heart.

Turning her head to avoid being caught staring, Sidney couldn't keep from watching Richard's movements. Such things as the way he raised his mug to drink his coffee or the way he held his pen. Even that funny thing he did with his mouth when he was in deep concentration. Richard bit the left side of his top lip when he was in deep thought. She wondered if realized it or not. Their awkward small talk continued until Sidney needed to head out to Brentwood. His kind words echoed in her mind for the duration of the day.

I haven't heard from Renée in a while, Richard mused. Dialing her number he realized it had been too long since the two of them had talked. It was not unusual for them to give each other a quick call during the day.

Buried in work, as usual, Renée could only speak briefly. Knowing this wasn't an ideal time; he did the next best thing and scheduled a phone call for that evening to catch up. Although brief, the conversation with his old friend chased his blue mood away.

∽

Looking up from a stack of papers, Richard saw Chelsea wheel Brian through the opened office doorway. "I'll be back in an hour, she said giving her husband a quick kiss.

"Brian. I didn't expect to see you today. How ya feelin'?"

"I felt better before I went to the doctor. I guess it's just all the moving around, but I'm doing fine. Thank the good Lord he cut most of my meds out. When this is all over, I never want to see another pill for the rest of my life." Richard and Brian shared a chuckle before they began discussing business.

"I'm curious, Rich. How's the lady plumber working out?"

"Very well," he said without hesitation. "She's here every day on time, hard worker, doing a great job. I haven't heard one complaint."

Brian was glad to hear good news about the new employee. He also asked about the other new hires. He wanted to know whom he could count on when he returned to the helm.

"You do realize when the company gets bigger you're going to have to hire more workers? Even though we hired two a few weeks ago, every employee is busy."

"Yes, I know," he replied while looking at a spreadsheet.

"Well, I'm headed out for some lunch. Want to join me? Or do you want to stay here and look at spreadsheets?" Richard asked.

"You go ahead. I want to read up on these numbers, and by then Chelsea will be back to take me home. I can't wait until I can drive myself. I think having to wait for someone to drive me everywhere has been the most aggravating thing about this whole situation."

"Catch ya later."

Richard left Brian to his spreadsheets and focused on where to eat lunch. Hungry but didn't want the hustle and bustle of a sit down restaurant, he drove up Broadway and pulled into Checkers. He ordered a burger and ate in his truck where he could be alone with his thoughts. The warm day made the small breeze welcoming as he watched the cars on the street go by. His head raced. Running Dunning Plumbing, Renée, his need for a future job and of course Caroline consumed him. Talking to Renée this morning reminded him of his apartment and friends in Atlanta.

Maybe I'll go home this weekend, Richard decided staring out the window. That's what I'll do. I'll go home and spend the whole weekend working on my résumé. In a few weeks Brian should be back in the office, so now's a good time. Wonder if Caroline is having lunch right now? Richard's train of thought was senseless. He went from résumés to Caroline in a split second. He wondered what she was doing and when she would be home. He wanted to call her so badly, but stopped himself. It was way too early in their semi-friendship, or whatever it was, to call too often. He would not be able to deal with it if she told him not to call again.

Later that evening, Renée called right on time. It was so good to hear her voice. He had missed his gal pal.

"Rich, how's it going?" She brought him up to date with her life. Richard could hear happiness in her voice. The two had fallen out of touch over the past several weeks, but they caught up quickly.

"It's going. I have just about got this office running more sufficiently. Could use a couple more workers, but I will let Brian deal with that when he gets back in the driver's seat. You'll love this one. We hired a woman plumber."

"You're kidding. I can't believe any woman would want to be a plumber."

Richard chuckled then continued to explain.

"When I got here, Brian was short on plumbers, so I interviewed a few people. And yes, one was a woman. But let me tell ya, this gal knows her stuff."

Uncertain of his timing, Richard asked about the new guy she had met a few weeks earlier. She answered nonchalantly.

"That turned out to be nothing. We're just friends and I seldom hear from him. But there is a new guy I've been seeing. His name is Stan, and I can't wait for you to meet him."

Renée and Richard talked about their jobs, family and new friends, but she felt there was something more that Richard wanted to discuss.

"Ok, Rich. What's up?"

"Oh, nothing, I just hadn't talked to you in a while and…I miss you. I miss our talks, I guess."

"You lie. There is something going on. I can hear it in your voice. If you were standing in front of me, I would probably see it on your face…so, let's cut to the chase and tell me what's up."

Renée knew Richard way better than he thought. He didn't lie totally. He did miss her and their friendship, but there was something eating at him and was unsure what it was. Or maybe he didn't want to admit what it was. Either way he wasn't sure.

He told her about Caroline. He shared how he met her and kept running into her in the oddest places. He revealed his desire to know her better and how much time he spent thinking about her. He was reluctant to tell her about going to church to see this woman, but took the leap. Renée couldn't believe it.

"But I really don't think she feels the same as I do."

"Let's recap a bit. You quit your job, go to your hometown to help your brother while he is laid up. And there you accidentally meet this woman. She doesn't give you any indication that she is interested, and she keeps popping up wherever you go. Then you go to a school reunion that you really didn't want to go to, but for whatever reason did and there she is...again. Turns out she's friends with one of your best friends and his wife. And I don't even know where to begin with you going to church. You've called her and it sounds like the two of you enjoyed talking to one another. Oh my dear Richard, it sounds to me like this is a case of a classic romantic love story."

"Oh, Renée," he whined drawing out her name in an unpleasant I-can't-believe-you-said-that tone.

Holding back a chuckle, Renée replied, "I'm serious. It really sounds like you finally met someone who has gotten all the way to your heart. Rich, you went to church for this woman! I've never known you to go to church for any reason. Let me ask you a question. Have you ever been in a serious romantic relationship ever?"

"I've dated several women."

"Not what I asked. Have you been serious about anyone, ever? I mean like, 'I want to keep seeing you forever? Or I can't wait to see you again' type of relationship?"

"Honestly, no. I don't think I have. Like I said, I've dated several women, but not for very long periods of time."

"Well, this woman has you on a new playing field. I think you may have finally met the one woman you could get serious with. And right now that has you confused because it has never happened before."

Richard listened to his friend, but was skeptical of whether or not her diagnosis was correct. He also never realized how well she knew him.

"And what about you? Have you ever had serious feelings for anyone before?"

Renée had to be careful how she responded since the answer would be very uncomfortable for both of them. She wanted to avoid the question all together, but he would never let her get away with that.

"Yes. But I realized early on it was not to be, so I kept my feelings to myself and we ended up being just friends."

"Well, that guy was a jerk. You have so much to offer and will make some man very happy some day."

There was silence for a few seconds, and Richard let out a sigh before he realized it.

"Well, oh great one, what should I do?"

"Simple. You have to figure out what it is you want. Enjoy it, Rich. Just don't go too fast. That is a mistake a lot of people make." Feeling uncomfortable Renée changed the conversation so she said the first thing that popped into her head.

"So, when are you coming back to Atlanta?"

"I may be back this weekend if I can get my paperwork caught up. I need to seriously work on finding a new job and updating my résumé. I have a few leads that I want to look into."

Renée was thrilled that her friend had plans to come home permanently. It was evident that she and Richard missed one another more than either realized. But for some reason Cupid never shot his arrow their way. They were friends, very close friends. After much heartache, Renée had accepted that.

❧ CHAPTER ELEVEN ❧

Richard spent the weekend in Atlanta as planned. Most of that time was spent in front of his computer refining his résumé. He did call Caroline a few times, and each time hated to hang up. He wondered if it was the same for her. Renée introduced Richard to Stan. The two seemed to hit it off fairly well. They invited Richard to come along with them to see a movie, but he declined thinking that it would be a little too weird. He was content being alone for the weekend. Before Sunday, Richard informed Renée that he should be back to stay within a month, maybe two. Pleased, even though she had a special someone right now, she wanted her bud back home where he belonged.

A week later, Brian hobbled into the office letting everyone know he would be coming in two, maybe three days a week for a few hours until released by his doctor. Relieved, Richard was ready to get back to his own life, despite not knowing his future.

The two brothers were engulfed in contracts, agreements and bids for new construction work. With bigger contracting jobs, new plumbers had been hired along with a full time office assistant. Brian's dream of expanding the family business was quickly turning into a reality. Katie now only came in to cover for someone when needed, but Todd continued to be in the office most days as usual. Construction was booming in middle Tennessee. With Richard's help, Brian felt he had a chance of getting in on the action. Thinking about Richard leaving and him flying solo made him a bit anxious. But anxiety or not, he was going for it.

One evening while having supper at his parents' home, the conversation concerning Richard's plans to go back to Atlanta came up. Richard had an answer for everyone who asked, but his answer to himself was always unclear.

"You sure you won't stay and work with your brother?" Todd asked his son while pouring sorghum molasses over his homemade biscuit.

"No, Dad, I think it's best to look for work elsewhere. I don't have plans to move from Atlanta, but I don't have anything keeping me there either. I guess you could say right now I'm a free agent." Richard chuckled, but suddenly Caroline's face came to mind. It was strange how her face would materialize totally out of the blue.

Todd let the matter drop. His children were grown adults now. They didn't need their daddy telling them what to do, and he refused to be that kind of parent. He had told each of them years ago he would always be there for them until the Lord took him home. He would help and advise them if needed, but he wouldn't interfere with their lives once they were grown adults.

For a brief moment, Richard wanted to ask his dad what he should do with his life. But he was a grown man. He had to make the choice himself. Richard caught himself remembering a time when his father possessed a different attitude about this subject. If he or his siblings were being "downright foolish", as his dad would say, he would simply tell them what they should do followed by reading them the riot act for being "downright foolish". He would then say, "I'm not raisin' no fools, so stop acting like it." Richard started to smile at the memory of his father's words.

"Oh, by the way, I saw George the other day. He said you dropped in for a visit at his church," Todd mentioned as the two walked into the living room.

"Yeah, Adam goes there."

"I'm glad you did. You need to get back in church, but that's something for you and the Lord to work out. I had to mention it though. If I didn't, your mother would let me know I should have."

Richard let out a laugh at his dad. "You know, Dad, ole George is a pretty good preacher, but I don't understand. Since you two are such good buddies why don't you and mom attend his church?"

"Because, son, your best buddy can't be you pastor, and your pastor can't be your best buddy. It just doesn't work that way. It's like this. If my good buddy was my pastor and one day we had a fallin' out, then not only have I lost my buddy, but I've lost my pastor too. On the other hand, if my pastor, who is also my good buddy, starts veering off on his preaching and I feel the need to leave that church, I've not only lost my pastor, but my good buddy as well. I've know several people who joined a church, got in a close friendship with the preacher and his family, and then something happened. And not only did the friendship end, but that family had to find a new church. George and I go back a long way. And when he began to preach we both agreed not to jeopardize that. But you're right, he is a good preacher."

The talk about preachers opened a floodgate of memories for Richard. He remembered a time when he and his siblings sat in church as children with their parents. Sometimes they would entertain themselves and get in trouble. These memories were pleasant. The faces of many Sunday school teachers paraded across Richard's mind leading him to wonder if any of them were still living. And if so, did they still attend church. Both Katie's and Brian's family still attended with their parents. Richard was the exception, and until recently he hadn't given church much thought.

"Whatcha thinkin', son?" Todd Dunning knew his children like the back of his hand. He knew when they were content and when they were trying to work something out. Currently, he knew his son was deep in thought.

"All this talk about you and George got me thinking about when we were kids and went to church. You and mom have gone to church forever, haven't ya, Dad?"

"Yes, and no. Your mother has, but I didn't until I was about fifteen. I had seen this beautiful gal. Oh my, she was pretty. I found out she went to church every Sunday. So I figured if I went there too, I could see her and maybe talk to her."

"Did it work?"

"I reckon so, she's in the kitchen." The two laughed out loud and Karen couldn't help but hear. "But then something happened. I couldn't keep the preacher's words from gettin' in my head, and then I realized why. I was a lost sinner, just like the Bible tells us. I asked Jesus to save me that summer. And then I no longer went just to see your momma, but to hear the Word. Been goin' ever since."

118

Todd wanted to know the real reason why his son no longer felt the need, or desire to be in the house of the Lord, but didn't want to put him on the defensive. But he wanted to take advantage of the opportunity to ask point blank since he had brought up the subject.

"What happened, son? Why did you stop goin'?"

Richard had to think for a moment. He knew the reason, but did he really want to rehash it? His mother came in to refill her husband's coffee cup, but quickly went back into the kitchen to work on the dishes when Richard answered.

"I don't know, Dad. After I got away from home, church was different. Then when I moved to Atlanta I went to this small church and got to know everybody. They got to know me, well, all except the preacher. For some reason he didn't try to get to know me…you know really know me. He made me feel like I was not good enough to be in his church. He asked my friends to do things like help take up the offering, play their instruments, teach a class, and stuff like that but never me. He wasn't right out rude to me, but looking back he was in a left-handed sort of way. One Sunday evening, he was preaching and made this comment about his sister and her family. He told us how they were raised the same, but he knew she was lost because she no longer went to church and lived her life differently than he did. I really don't think that was right of him. Not only to judge his sister, but to berate her from the pulpit like that. Then later, he verbally slandered the dad of one of my friends who was very faithful in that church. He was kind of quiet and kept to himself, but he was a nice guy. And the preacher just went after him for some reason, and it got back to my friend's dad. It hurt him deeply. And to this day I don't think either of them go to church anymore. That man had no right, Dad, no right at all to judge those people like that. I don't know. Since then I just lost all interest in going. I doubt church will ever be the same for me."

Todd's heart ached as he listened to his son. He also never wanted to punch a preacher in the nose before in all his life like he did at that moment. This man had destroyed something he and his wife had worked a lifetime to build and instill in their children. Todd picked up his cup and took a long drink, praying quickly for the Lord to give him the right words for his son.

"You're right, Richard. Preacher or not, that man had no right to publicly judge those people like that. The Bible teaches us a series of steps that is the right way for Christians to confront one another of sin, and he didn't follow that. Judging each other in that way is not for any of us to do, and he will answer to the Lord for that. This man has caused you to stumble, but you cannot stay down. You have to get up. As he will answer for his actions, you will answer for yours. You were right to leave that church, but your choice to stay out is not the correct response."

Richard heard his father's words knowing they came from his heart, but it would take days for those words to actually sink in and affect him.

The week seemed to drag on for Richard. Unproductive and unfocused at work he had a difficult time moving through the days. He almost wrecked his truck. His relationship with

Caroline was only on a phone call level which Richard definitely wanted to change. He wanted to spend time with her.

Friday morning, Adam called to invite Richard to play some basketball with a few other guys. As he accepted, he figured that could be just what the doctor ordered. Running up and down a basketball court could help burn his frustration or whatever it was out of his system while trying to put a ball through the hoop.

"Sounds great! See ya there," Adam said ending his call.

Richard picked up his phone to call his brother. Brian would benefit from the evening out as well.

"I know you can't play, but it will be good for you to get out somewhere other than to the office and the doctor." Brian happily agreed and brought his young teenage son Brett also.

At six o'clock Friday evening, the group showed up at one of the local community centers ready to play. They were excited just like little boys only taller and with five o'clock shadows.

Adam introduced Richard to Matt and Allen, and like most guys he didn't have any problem playing basketball with someone he didn't know. Brett was content to sit and watch the others play, but the guys were in agreement that Brett would sub when someone needed a rest. He agreed and ended up playing more than anyone else did.

Richard played hard successfully working out his frustration. Sprinting fast up and down the court, passing the ball and taking shots felt wonderful, but his body was telling him he had lost his mind.

Sitting on the sidelines taking a breather, Richard noticed Brian looked like he was enjoying himself too. He wondered which one of the Dunning brothers needed this the most.

"So when do you get your cast off?"

"Ten days, four hours and twelve minutes." Richard couldn't help but laugh out loud.

"Okaay."

A few moments passed when Brian broke the silence. "Who is she, Richard?"

"What?"

"Who is she? I've noticed you being in a mood little brother. Heck, we all have noticed. There has to be only one reason for a man getting in such a state as you have been in the last several weeks, and that's a woman. Now, who is she?"

"Doesn't matter, probably nothing will come of it. So I'd just rather drop the subject if you don't mind."

Brian felt victorious over discovering it was a woman that had Richard all twisted up inside, but respected his brother's wishes and turned the conversation back to the game. Richard went back out onto the floor while Adam took a break. Yes, this was the best medicine for Richard's ailment.

❧ CHAPTER TWELVE ❧

While drinking his morning coffee, Richard sat at the table in his bathrobe bare footed pondering his next move. Do I go or not? If I go, then I need to get dressed. If not, I can sit here all day and it won't matter. Jake walked into the kitchen and headed for his favorite cereal.

"Jake, I have a question for you. What would you think if a girl you knew that didn't go to your church came to your church and sat with you? Would you think she came just to see you?"

"Well, duh," Jake said before filling his mouth with cereal.

Looking at his nephew chewing a mouth full of cereal, Richard knew that was the extent of his answer.

"Thanks, man. I knew I could count on you for an honest answer."

With the help of his nephew, Richard decided not to attend church today, Instead he drove to his normal Sunday morning happy place. Heavy in thought he sat in Krispy Kreme eating a strawberry-filled doughnut. Suddenly, without invitation, his father's words from a few days ago came bursting through his thoughts. A preacher had caused him to stop going to church, and Richard had allowed that person to keep him out. As he thought on this, he felt uncomfortable with the issue. He responded by putting more effort on focusing on his newspaper, but failed. Looking at his watch he realized if he left right now, he could make it before Brother Whitehurst began his morning sermon.

Walking in just as the congregation was sitting down after the last song, Richard scanned the room for Caroline. She was sitting right in front of Adam and Sabrina, but her pew was pretty much full. Squeezing in was not an option and would be rude. The next best choice was to sit with Adam and Sabrina who had the pew almost to themselves. Casually he made his way to where they sat. As he passed over knees and legs, he casually took his finger and tickled the back of Caroline's neck giving her a shiver. Turning, she saw a familiar handsome man smiling mischievously at her causing her a different kind of shiver.

Brother Whitehurst began his message. And once again, Richard struggled to remain focused on his words. Not bored by the speaker, it was simply that Richard was distracted by the lovely head of light brown hair in front of him. Oh how he wanted to reach out and touch Caroline's gorgeous hair, but knowing it would get him in trouble if he did.

Suddenly Richard's attention shifted from Caroline's hair to the pastor's voice resonating across the sanctuary. Brother Whitehurst words on a pastor's responsibility to his flock caused Richard to think. He had undoubtedly been negatively affected by a pastor's wrongdoing, but recently had been confronted about his response to it. Even though several years had passed, Richard continued to cling to his negative feelings by not moving forward in his relationship with the Lord. This revelation sank deep into his heart and he knew it was time he dealt with it. It would be many hours later when lying in bed Richard would finally talk to the Lord about his response to that wrong doing.

The final amen was said signaling the people to gather their things while the kids raced off in all different directions as if there was a fire somewhere. Richard stood gazing at Caroline as she turned around to collect her purse and Bible.

"Hello, Richard. Glad you could make it today."

"Thank you. Is your son here too?" He asked looking around the room.

"Yes, Joshua is with the other teens. They all gather in one place and talk after the service. Sometimes he sits with me and sometimes he sits with them."

Adam interrupted the conversation between these two. "Hey, Sabrina and I are going to grab a bite to eat at O'Charley's. You two want to join us?"

"Oh, thank you, Adam, but Joshua and I are expected at my brother's today for dinner. Maybe some other time."

"I'm free, so I'm in. This way Sabrina will have some good conversation at the dinner table for once." Richard gave his friend a slap on the back and a big hearty laugh.

"See ya at the restaurant, buddy."

Adam and Sabrina left the other two thinking they needed some privacy.

"Sorry you can't make it. I was looking forward to having Sunday dinner with you."

Not really knowing how to respond, she covered quite nicely. "Yeah, that would be nice. We'd join you if I hadn't already told my brother we were coming."

Many conversations buzzed all around them. Standing with just a pew between them, Caroline could only hear Richard's voice and was captivated by its sound.

∞

Richard felt the heat and humidity of middle Tennessee. Sitting on the porch swing overlooking the backyard at his sister's, he took a long drink of his iced tea and welcomed the coolness inside his body. Originally he had planned to be here for the shortest time possible, but something had changed. Now, he wasn't sure if he wanted to leave or not. The reason was due to a stunning woman with the most beautiful blue eyes. When she looked at him, the man turned to mush.

After supper, Richard's restlessness wasn't helped by the warm weather. He had to do something, go somewhere. "Anyone up for Sonic?" he called out from the middle of the living room.

Ashley and Jake were his only takers which was fine. He enjoyed these two very much. He loved listening to them banter and bicker with each other. At times it reminded him of his own siblings. While ordering milkshakes he heard a voice coming from the other side of the menu board. While he could not see a face, he knew the voice. That voice had been the reason for his sleepless nights, the many unproductive days, and the utter confusion about what was going on inside his mind.

When Richard finished his order, he poked his head around to find the face that went with the voice. Not saying a word, Richard smiled broadly at the enchanting person connected to the voice.

"Richard. Hi."

"Hello. Come here often?" he chuckled.

"Actually, yes I do. About twice a week," Caroline said, laughing. "Are you alone?"

"No, I have my niece and nephew with me. What about you?"

"I'm alone. Joshua is working until close this evening, and I had to work late myself. I just finished my shift. So I'm being bad and grabbing a burger and fries for my supper."

"Then you can join us." Richard introduced his niece and nephew to Caroline. The orders came out quickly. Milkshakes for Richard, Ashley and Jake, but Caroline had a full meal. As the shakes were being passed around, he searched his mind desperately for something intelligent to say, but of course was met with nothing.

Caroline, Ashley and Jake eased into friendly conversation smoothly leaving Richard a bit behind. Suddenly, hitting him like a brick dropping on his head, Richard realized why. *She has a teenage son, stupid.* The little group had been chatting for nearly two hours when Caroline's cell rang. It was her father. Seeing who it was she took the call but kept it brief. Richard really didn't want to leave, but knew they should. They clearly were finished and kept others from using the table.

"Well, I really need to be going," Caroline said. "Thank you for inviting me to eat with you. Otherwise I would have taken it home and eaten alone. Richard, I'll be talking to you later. Ashley, Jake it was great meeting you two."

"Yeah, you too," they said in unison.

Richard watched Caroline walk to her car and eventually drive off. His niece and nephew noticed and looked at each other with a grin on their faces.

"Yo, Uncle Richard," his nephew said in a ribbing sing-song tone. Both kids started giggling and teasing their uncle. "You got yourself a girlfriend?"

"Now, what makes you say that?" Richard shot back thinking he had done nothing to give himself away.

The two kids shared a look and snickered again. "Well, the way you kept looking at her and the fact that we finished our shakes about half an hour ago."

"Yeah, Uncle Rich has a girlfriend," Jake sang again.

At nine-thirty unable to resist any longer, Richard called Caroline. Sonic had never been so enjoyable as it was this evening with her. He feared her rejection, but he also knew he couldn't keep spinning his wheels and going nowhere. It's my job to make the first move, not hers. Richard...dude, time to fish or cut bait, he concluded.

Richard was about to hang up when Caroline picked up on the fifth ring. She had just stepped out of the shower and was wrapped in a towel.

"Hello," she said a little breathless.

"Caroline, this is Richard. Are you alright?"

"Yes. I had to hurry to get to the phone," she said trying to hold her towel together.

"Caroline, I know we just spent two hours talking at Sonic, but there is something I want to ask you, and I didn't want to do that in front of my niece and nephew. I have really enjoyed talking to you and getting to know you, but I would like to get to know you more. I guess what I'm trying to say, but doing a horrible job of it, is will you go out on a date with me this weekend?"

Caroline didn't know what to say. She sat gripping her towel tighter and tighter as if it were her lifeline. She really wished she could put Richard on hold to call Melissa or rewind their conversation to before he asked. Being silly and unrealistic, she knew she could do neither. She did enjoy talking to him as well. He too had invaded her thoughts a few times and was certainly nice to look at. So why was she so hesitant with this guy? She had spent more years than she cared to count avoiding men. Now this one was not only on the phone but in her head also. She could no longer avoid him.

"Aah, well, maybe that would be fine if you don't mind coming here on Saturday to have supper with me and Joshua."

Not what Richard had expected but it would be acceptable. "Sounds great, can I bring anything?"

"No...no. That won't be necessary. Will six-thirty be too early for you?

"Six-thirty is fine."

Richard had a scheduled date for this Saturday evening. Just the thought of being on a date with her made him feel on top of the world.

Saturday morning before Joshua left for work, he watched his mother clean the house like a woman on a mission. When he asked why she was deep cleaning everything, she reminded him, "We are having a guest this evening, remember?" To Caroline that answered the question. To her teenage son it did not. But what she didn't tell him was cleaning was keeping her mind off of the fact that she had a date this evening.

Normally on Saturdays Joshua worked three to close, but she had asked him to see if he could rearrange his schedule to be home by six. Since the night before, Caroline's mind had been overloaded with the menu, her outfit and the condition of the house. Joshua just sat there not knowing what to say. He had never seen her in such a state.

"Joshua, if you don't like him or if any of this upsets you in any way, I will tell him we cannot see each other and that will be the end of it. I need you to tell me your true feelings on this matter no matter what they are," she said, almost begging. Caroline had seen many families destroyed due to a new spouse or special friend in the family, and she refused to allow that to happen. "Is that totally clear, Joshua?"

"Yeah, Mom, I got it." Joshua was unsure how he felt about this situation. His mother had never dated anyone before, at least not that he could remember.

It was exactly six-thirty when Richard arrived carrying a dozen soft pink roses. It was his niece's idea, a good one, now that he thought about it.

Hearing a knock on the front door, Caroline forced herself to stop fidgeting with her hands as she walked toward the sound to let her date in. Stopping just short of the door, she took a deep breath and let it out slowly.

"Hi, come on in."

"Hi, these are for you. Beautiful flowers for a beautiful lady." She slowly accepted the gift as a bit of color came to her face, close to the color of the roses.

Caroline smiled as she put the roses to her nose and took in their wonderful aroma. "Mmm, there is something about roses….isn't there? Thank you, Richard. They're lovely."

Joshua walked in the room just after Caroline finished smelling the roses. He was now very curious about the man who had his mother so uptight about being in their home.

"I think you've already met my son Joshua." Extending his hand, Joshua gave Richard a firm handshake letting him know he was not a boy but a man, and the man of this house.

"Supper is almost ready. Please sit down and make yourself comfortable. I have sweet tea made. Would you like a glass now or would you rather wait?"

"I think I'll wait if that is ok." Richard would have loved to have had a glass at that moment because his throat was a bit dry. But due to his nerves he was afraid he would spill it. Joshua took the recliner and Richard the sofa, neither one knowing what to say. Breaking the uncomfortable silence, Joshua turned on the TV luckily finding a news anchorman reporting the only part of the news either one of them watched, the sports report. This seemed to ease the awkwardness between the two and they quickly began talking about their favorites. Richard learned that Joshua liked sports as much as the next teenager, and that he was a huge fan of the Nashville Predators. He could recite every player's stats and their history with other leagues. As this conversation continued, Joshua also revealed that the Tennessee Vols was his favorite basketball team. Caroline called the two guys to the table. After the blessing was said, the talk of sports continued.

"Looks like you two found something to talk about," Caroline commented as she began serving. Richard smiled, but Joshua's only focus at the moment was his plate.

"Yeah. It seems we like a few of the same teams."

Caroline made the classic southern dinner of fried chicken, mashed potatoes with peas and carrots and homemade biscuits on the side. She topped it off with ice cream for dessert.

"There is nothing like a home cooked meal. Since I've been staying with my sister's family I've put on a little weight from eating Katie's home cookin'. Being a bachelor, I normally work long hours and grab something on the way home. The only thing I can actually cook is pasta. Anything else is heat-and-eat.

"We don't eat like this every night, but when we do, we like it don't we, Mom?"

"Yes, Joshua." Caroline was slightly embarrassed. She didn't want her guest to think she rarely cooked. She smiled at her son as he spooned potatoes in his mouth.

"Next Saturday, my sister's family and I are going out on their boat. Would you care to join us? Of course, I mean you too, Joshua. My niece and nephew will be there, and they are close to your age. We usually take a cooler of food and drinks and go tubing. You know, just have fun and relax out on the water."

"Awww that sounds great, can we Mom? I can ask off for next Saturday. Can we?"

Caroline found it almost amusing that this man whom she would barely speak to in the hardware store now sat at the other end of her table eating a meal she had prepared for him. Such a handsome face and warm eye, she mused. Shocked she quickly shook herself back into reality. "Aah...I... aah I don't think we have any plans for next Saturday."

"Great! So we can go?" Joshua eagerly asked.

"Sure. Sounds wonderful."

What are you doing? She heard herself frantically say inside her head. Caroline was starting to feel pressured. Nothing had changed. She still wasn't looking for a romantic relationship, but wasn't so sure right now. After spending several hours on the phone, at the reunion and at Sonic, and now having him over for dinner, her judgment was clouded and unclear.

Richard lay in bed replaying the evening. Joshua seemed to be comfortable around him after finding common ground in sports. Although thankful for the boating event Russ and Katie had put together, he would much rather be alone with Caroline on a relaxing day at the lake. But he would take what he could get. Suddenly Richard considered his job issues. What about Atlanta? I don't have a job lined up. What woman wants to date a man who is out of work? I'm not out of work. I'm working for Brian. What if I cannot find a job after he returns? These thoughts plagued Richard.

❧ CHAPTER THIRTEEN ❧

Monday morning, Richard headed to work like usual, except for the traffic jam on the interstate. This stop in his morning routine allowed him time to listen to his thoughts once again. His mind was never far from Caroline. Sitting in a long line of cars with a grin on his face, he could not believe he was actually considering staying in middle Tennessee. But the time he had spent with Caroline made it sound reasonable. Spending time with her made anywhere sound reasonable.

Melissa couldn't wait to get the details about Caroline's date with Richard. When Caroline told her about the invitation to go boating, she was thrilled for her friend. The outing sounded fun, but Caroline contained her excitement within herself. She revealed to Melissa that she couldn't seem to stop accepting his invitations.

"It's the craziest thing, Melissa. I've told myself over and over I will not go out with him. And the next thing I know I have a dinner date with him. Now I've accepted an invitation to go boating."

Melissa could easily tease her friend about this, and one day would, but for now, it was too serious for Caroline. "Just remember to go slow. And so far, I think you have been."

❧

The day had finally arrived. Richard had an all-day date with Caroline. So what if her son, his sister, brother-in-law, niece and nephew were going to be there as well? He would get to spend the whole day being around this woman who was wreaking havoc on his heart.

Richard got up at six-fifteen to start preparing for the day. He made a quick trip to Kroger for ice, soft drinks and other things they might need. As he shopped, Richard forecasted the day's fun. Suddenly stopping in his tracks while standing in front of the suntan lotion, for the first time he wondered what Caroline would be wearing on the boat. The plan for the day was boating, tubing and having fun on the lake, so a bathing suit would be appropriate. The thought of Caroline in a bathing suit caused him to come to a complete stop. The man stood frozen right there in the aisle in front of the Banana Boat lotion.

"Excuse me," a young lady said with her cart loaded with groceries and two children.

"Huh? Oh, I'm…I'm sorry." Richard shifted his cart so the lady could pass. He softly shook his head bringing himself back to reality. He finished his shopping and drove back to his sister's home.

"Richard, are you alright?" Katie asked noticing her brother acting a little strange.

"What? Oh, yeah…fine…I'm fine."

Katie looked at her brother as she continued packing their food for their day on the lake when she started to grin.

"What?"

"Nothing," she said as she kept grinning.

"Kathryn, what are you laughing at me about?"

"So tell me about this lady you've met. Caroline?" she answered trying to control her grinning.

"Yes, her name is Caroline." At that moment, Richard looked pitifully vulnerable. "Katie, help me out here. And if you laugh at me, I will get you back, just remember that. Do you think if I offer for Joshua to ride with Ashley and Jake, it might give the wrong impression?"

"You mean like, 'hey that guy just wants me out of the way so he can be alone with my mom impression'? Yeah, you might want to hold off on that offer this time."

Caroline and Joshua pulled up to Katie and Russ' house around nine. Richard had been impatiently watching for them like a kid waiting for the ice cream truck.

"Hi, have any trouble finding the place?" he asked as they were getting out of the car.

"No, I knew pretty close to where it was. It's a beautiful home," she said gazing at the house.

Dressed in trunks, tee shirt and flip-flops Joshua looked like any normal teenage guy going on a boat. Caroline, however, with her hair pulled up loosely with a clip wore a bright teal colored cover up. To Richard, it appeared to be a simple sleeveless, short dress. What he didn't know was that underneath she wore a matching one-piece bathing suit.

"Oh, Joshua, sweetie, would you get the cooler out of the trunk please?" Joshua turned to do as asked.

"Oh, Caroline, you didn't need to bring anything. I have it all covered."

"I know, but I had a watermelon in the fridge, so I cut it up and brought it. Cold fruit on a hot day is so refreshing."

Richard took Caroline and Joshua inside and introduced them to his family. Caroline was a bit nervous, but not to the point where it made her ill. Russ and Katie were eager to meet her, especially Katie. She had never seen her brother act like this. Even during his teenage years, he had never acted this way over a girl. After the introductions were made, easy conversation began settling Caroline's nerves. Then Katie quickly concluded what captivated her brother.

Briefly finding a private moment, Katie caught Richard by the shirt and spoke where only he could hear. "Richard, she is adorable." Richard could not control the sparkle in his eyes or the grin that spread across his face.

They all piled into two vehicles to head to the lake. Russ, Katie and the kids pulled the boat while Richard, Caroline and Joshua followed behind in Katie's car. Not wanting Caroline to feel cramped, Richard asked to drive his sister's car, and with a grin she handed him the keys.

Arriving at Old Hickory Lake and seeing several boaters already on the water, the men backed the boat down the ramp and launched it into the Lake. Jake and Joshua busied themselves loading the coolers and collecting life jackets. Ashley removed her oversized T-shirt and put her life jacket on over her one-piece bathing suit, while Katie and Caroline remained in their cover-ups. Richard was relieved. Making a total idiot of himself was the last thing he wanted to do today. His niece and nephew hopped in the back of the boat and called for Joshua to join them.

The laughter echoed around Old Hickory Lake as each person took turns tubing. Russ and Richard each got into a tube while Katie drove the boat. Hilarity began as they pushed off the other's tube with their feet causing them to ricochet off each other. At one point, Russ was actually flipped out of his tube after being bumped and bounced off a wave resulting in an uproar of laughter.

By two o'clock, everyone was starved. The ladies opened the coolers and effortlessly put together lunch in minutes. A tasty meal of ham and turkey sandwiches was a blessing to all. Each ate their fill while enjoying the gentle breeze coming off the water. Jake and his hollow legs ate nearly a whole can of Pringles chips by himself. His mother had to put the brakes on his attack on the watermelon since it would be needed later for a refreshing snack. And of course no one could resist Katie's homemade chocolate chip cookies to complete the spread.

"Joshua, let's swim around the boat," Jake suggested.

"Hey, I want to come," Ashley chimed in.

Jake was ready to jump off the back of the boat when Russ's voice caused him to stop and turn around.

"Jake. No diving off the boat. You have just eaten lunch. You need to wait a while before going back in the water, especially after eating as much as you did."

Gently bobbing in the water, the adults chatted as they enjoyed cold soft drinks while the three teens occupied themselves waiting for time to pass. Finally, Jake heard his dad ask, "Ladies, neither of you have been in the tube. Caroline, want to give it a try?" Even though she thought it looked like fun, she declined. She didn't think doing something daring like tubing was the best thing to do when initially meeting someone's family for the first time. Katie passed as well. She didn't want to put any pressure on Caroline.

"Maybe next time," Caroline responded.

Next time. She said next time! Her words rang in Richard's ears and made him one happy man.

After a couple more hours of playing on the lake, the group was getting tired. The sun was getting lower signaling the end of the day. They huddled around the cooler and devoured the cool, juicy watermelon. Finishing they began to pack up and this brought moans from the tireless teens. It had been a long, festive day on the water and in the sun. Everyone looked windburned, but only Ashley had a little pink across her nose from the sun.

On the drive back, Joshua fell asleep right away and Caroline was feeling a little tired herself, but Richard seemed to have plenty of energy. He glanced briefly over at her and smiled. Looking in his rearview mirror, he could see that Joshua was out cold. He spoke softly for only Caroline to hear.

"I'm so glad you and Joshua came today," he said taking his hand and laying it gently over hers. His touch struck a chord in her that took her by surprise.

"Thank you for the invite. We both enjoyed ourselves very much." She turned and glanced at Joshua's sleeping form in the back seat. "I believe my son is exhausted from all the enjoyment," she continued with a hint of laugher.

Richard pulled into the driveway around eight-thirty, just minutes after Russ and Katie. Joshua woke up and began to put his shoes on.

Caroline insisted she and Joshua help unload everything, Richard didn't want her to, but she told him "Many hands make light work." In less than half an hour, both vehicles were unloaded and the gear stored back into the garage.

"Ok, Joshua, I think we're ready. Russ, Katie, thank you again for having us."

"Oh, Caroline, it was our pleasure. Please come back anytime," Katie responded sincerely.

Heading toward the doorway, Richard put his hand on the small of Caroline's back to walk her and Joshua to their car. She was certainly aware of his touch. Being every bit the gentleman, he opened the door for her. He was disappointed to see this wonderful day come to an end.

"Richard, we had so much fun being around you and your family today. I like them."

"Yeah, I think they like you too. I know Jake and Ashley liked Joshua, no doubt there." Joshua was already in the car, so Richard took advantage of the opportune moment and gave Caroline a gentle kiss on the cheek.

On the drive home, Caroline's mind was on Richard. Joshua's mind on the other hand was on his empty stomach and asked to stop for a burger. She thought of Richard's hand touching hers and could still feel his gentle kiss on her cheek. Such a simple but effective display of emotion, she was sure he had no idea what effect it was having on her.

Joshua showered and hit the bed within fifteen minutes. Caroline moved a bit slower. She wanted to call Melissa, but her head was in the clouds. There was no way she could keep the conversation short, which would cause her to shower too late. Melissa would have to wait until tomorrow.

As Caroline stood in the shower tilting her head back, she wiped the water away from her face. Questions flooded her mind without permission and without answers. Did she want a serious relationship to develop with Richard? What if he wanted more from her than she could give? More 'what if' queries continued. Caroline experienced a barrage of emotions. Excitement and fear of a potentially romantic relationship and the confusion on what to do about it seemed to be her primary concerns.

Slipping into her nightgown, she glimpsed over at the clock. Ten-thirty was definitely too late to call Melissa, but it was impossible for her to fall asleep with so much on her mind. Watching TV until she felt sleepy usually worked, but not tonight. She watched one show after another until finally at two-eighteen she turned it off, only to toss and turn.

The noise that was invading her recently found sleep wasn't in her dreams. Trying to open her eyes she realized it was her alarm clock going off. Finding the sound without fully opening her stinging eyes, Caroline made it stop and returned to her slumber until a tapping on her door fully woke her.

"Mom, are you not going to church today?"

"Huh, what?...Oh...I must of turned off my alarm and went back to sleep. I didn't fall asleep until way in the morning, so I'm not going to make it today. But you can go ahead. Really I'm fine."

Joshua finished getting ready and then let his mom know he was leaving and would bring home lunch.

At eleven-twenty, Caroline woke up feeling a little more rested. She detested nights like that, but was thankful this one had not occurred on a night when she had to get up for work the next day.

Joshua returned home with lunch as promised. He picked up one of his favorites, KFC with all the fixin's. Caroline had just finished dressing and was about to set the table when he walked in. She quickly grabbed some drinks and sat down to a lovely lunch and conversation.

"Eric and Heather may come over later and bring a movie. I told them that was ok. It is ok, isn't it?"

"Yes, it's ok, but it is best to ask first."

"Oh, Mr. Dunning was at church today and he was asking about you. Mom, is he gonna be hanging around now?"

"Joshua, honey, I don't know. Would that be a bad thing... if he came around?"

"I don't know," Joshua's mind suddenly clicking into high gear. "He wants to be more than friends, doesn't he?"

"I think so, and I want to make sure that is totally ok with you. 'Cause if it's not, then it's not ok with me."

Taking a big bite of chicken, Joshua looked at his mother and realized for the first time in his life a man was interested in his mom. It felt weird.

"I will only be ok with it if you are. But if I think he is wrong for you, can I tell you?"

"Absolutely, I want you to tell me the moment you feel that way...promise?"

"Promise."

Neither of them had meant for the subject to come up, but Joshua felt more at ease knowing he could tell his mother his true feelings about Richard whatever the reason. Caroline was relieved after their little chat as well. With that out of the way, she could not ignore her desire to know what Richard had said to Joshua earlier at church.

It was intriguing to learn that Richard had been to her church other than the one time when he tickled the back of her neck. Her curiosity rose wondering if he was there because of his friends, of her or of his need to be at church.

"You said Richard was at church this morning?"

"Yeah, he said to tell you hello." Caroline glanced at her son from across the table and watched as he filled his mouth with food. She instantly had unspoken questions she wanted to rapidly fire at her son. And that's it? That's all he said? Surely he said more than that. Why do teenage boys not repeat all that was said when asked to? She then settled on, "Did he say anything else?"

"Uh, just hi." This was clearly all Caroline was getting out of Joshua on this subject. However, her own thoughts surprised her. Wonder if he is eating with his family today? We could be eating Sunday dinner together if I hadn't had such a rough night. She was going to have to come to terms with her feelings for Richard Dunning, much sooner than later.

Caroline had just finished clearing the table and cleaning the kitchen when the phone rang and someone knocked on the door at the same time.

"Well….goodness. Joshua, will you get the phone while I get the door, please?"

Joshua's friends were at the door, and Richard was on the phone for Caroline. It made for an interesting Sunday afternoon. Eric, Heather and Jana arrived with a movie in hand along with some shakes from Sonic. Caroline took her phone call in her room so she could have some privacy and not interrupt the movie.

"I hope I didn't keep you out too late last night."

"No, don't be silly. Why would you ask that?"

"Well, Joshua was at church today, but you were not. He said you didn't get much sleep last night." In all actuality, he was selfishly hoping he was the subject of her sleepless night.

"He was right, I didn't, but it was not because I was out too late. Sometimes I will have one of those nights where I just cannot go to sleep. Ever have those, Richard?"

If you only knew, his mind answered followed by his voice. "Oh, yeah. And I hate those nights. No matter what I do to correct the problem the only thing that works is the sun getting close to coming up."

Laughing at his comments on sleep deprivation and agreeing on how true the statement was, Caroline repeatedly found herself content with talking and listening to this interesting man. How this all started, she could not say, but here she was, lying across the bed like a teenager and talking on the phone with a person who made her feel alive.

Richard and Caroline spent three hours on the phone talking about every subject from family to workplace until she realized it was time to get ready for church. He had not thought about attending the evening services, but now, hearing that she would be there he suddenly felt the urge to go.

∞

As the services neared, Joshua sat with a few of his friends on the same pew where he and his mom could be found every week. Caroline joined her son but sat a little father down. As she settled into her seat, she casually glanced around the congregation making sure it was not obvious to anyone that she was specifically looking for someone. Several people along with Adam and Sabrina arrived at the last minute. She nonchalantly scanned the room to see if Richard was one of those people.

"Good evening, everyone. It's so good to see you back tonight. And if you were not here this morning, I'm glad you are here now. David, come and lead us in a song of praise."

Richard walked in while Brother Whitehurst was finishing up the announcements. Everyone else was seated and he automatically went to sit beside Caroline hoping he was not causing an uncomfortable situation for anyone. Turning her head to see who was coming up beside her, she saw him wearing that smile that made her melt.

The song service was the same as it was on Sunday morning, booming and very lifting for the soul. Richard was enveloped by it. Even if he really wasn't in touch with his spiritual needs right now, he felt something stirring inside him. At this point in Richard's life, many things divided his attention, he didn't think he had time or space for one more.

David had the congregation turn and shake hands with one another. When Caroline turned to shake Richard's already extended hand, they looked into each other's eyes, both wearing the same smile. Neither could keep from it, she just hoped no one else noticed.

"I'm glad you could make it," she said.

"I'm glad you are here this time," he teased, causing them both to laugh.

Not giving anyone else the chance to shake their hands, the banter continued. "I also wasn't for sure if I should sit beside you or not. I hope it's ok. When Adam and I sit together we get into trouble." This caused Caroline to let out another soft laugh at the silliness. She pictured the two grown men acting up in church. Suddenly a loud voice called everyone's attention back into the service.

"If you would please take your Bibles and let's feed on God's word, shall we? But first, let's go to our Heavenly Father and ask His blessings on the preaching service.

"Dear Heavenly Father, I come to you asking for you guidance as I stand before these people, your people, Father. Fill my mouth with only your words, forbid me to mislead them even in my ignorance. I'm just a man who needs to be filled with you. Help us to receive your word and let no one leave this room this evening, Father, without knowing you. In Jesus' precious name I pray. Amen."

The peaceful stillness of everyone sitting at the same time quietly whooshed over the auditorium as Brother Whitehurst began his sermon.

"Tonight I want to speak to you about you. Sounds a little odd, doesn't it? But God laid this message on my heart a few days ago, and well, here it comes. If you don't like it, I suggest you take it up with Him, and then the two of you can work that out."

Even though there was a bit of seriousness in what Brother Whitehurst said, there was also a hint of humor. The light laughter was heard coming from the congregation.

"It's summer right now. School is out and people are taking vacations. We seem to be more relaxed during the summer months, or at least I think so. I have a simple question that I want you to answer in your own mind and heart. But be honest, because remember, God already knows the truth. Now, here is the question I want each of us, including myself to answer…"

Caroline had Richard so distracted. She invaded his thoughts at work, while driving on the road, watching sports, and now in a church. He would be pleased to know at this moment he was distracting to her as well. Caroline was very aware of his presence, but hoped her feelings weren't revealed on her face.

Someone near Richard coughed abruptly bringing him out of his daydreams and back to the man speaking. He shifted in his seat and tried to refocus.

"…We are told by God in Genesis to remember the Sabbath day and to keep it holy. Is that your answer? If so, there really should be more."

Quickly sliding back to his daydreaming, I'm going to ask her out after the service. We can go out for ice cream or something, yeah, maybe go to Sonic or… A little boy sitting in front of Richard needed to go out, so Richard was once again brought back to the Pastors words.

"…our reasons for coming to the Lord's house should be to worship Him, to learn more about Him, to have a closer relationship with Him. You see, it should always be about Him." Brother Whitehurst closed his Bible and paused briefly before speaking again. "Pray with me, please."

Joshua was headed to Eric's house to play video games after the service, and naturally, they planned to grab a burger on the way. Adam asked Richard if he would like to go with them to Shoney's for dessert or something. He asked his friend to hold that thought for a moment. Turning to Caroline, he extended an invitation and without hesitation she agreed.

"Ya know, one of these days I'm gonna get to go out on a date with you alone," Richard spoke softly in Caroline's ear. She remained silent, but did give him a smile. Then as quick as a wink a master plan formed in his mind.

"How about Joshua takes your car to his friend's house, giving him his own way home, and you ride with me to Shoney's. I promise to get you home safe and sound."

There was that smile again, "I think that would work if you're sure you don't mind." That sounded even ridiculous to her own ears. Of course he didn't mind.

While sitting around a large table at Shoney's, Caroline learned that Richard loved almost every sport known to man, cared deeply for his family, and was possibly going back to Atlanta soon. She didn't know how she felt about that last little tidbit of information. As the chatter continued she immediately thought, If he goes back to Atlanta, I won't be seeing him. He could still call, but he won't be here. A sudden sadness took her by surprise.

Unaware she was doing so, Caroline circled the top of her glass with her index finger. This friendship with Richard Dunning definitely unnerved her.

As Joshua got out of his car, Richard and Caroline pulled in the driveway behind him. He turned to meet them.

"Did you enjoy your dessert at Shoney's?"

"Yes, we did. How was your burger from Sonic?" Caroline responded.

"Fine, and so was the shake," he said smiling and rubbing his stomach.

❧ CHAPTER FOURTEEN ❧

Thursday morning, Brian received clearance from his doctor to return to work full- time. Having the accident behind him was a relief. He could finally move forward. Over the past two weeks, Richard made an effort to distance himself from the staff and the majority of the office responsibilities to make the transition a bit easier. But his future ultimately concerned him. He needed to decide whether to stay here or go back to Atlanta. It really all depended on Caroline and the direction of their relationship.

Richard stopped what he was doing to look at his watch and then called Caroline hoping to catch her on her lunch hour.

"Hey you."

"Hey yourself," she responded.

"I had a few minutes. Thought I would call you while you were on your lunch break. I want to ask you out on a date. A just the two of us date."

"I'll have to check my social calendar," she joked as she took a sip of her soft drink. "Looks like I'm free. What did you have in mind?"

"How about dinner and a movie? Or a movie and then dinner?"

"Either one of those sounds fine."

"Good, then I will see you around six."

"See ya then."

Caroline couldn't remember the last movie she had seen in a theater. She and Melissa went occasionally if there was one they both wanted to see. They each had distinctive tastes in movies, so it was rare they went. The last one they saw together was too creepy for Caroline and she spent most of the time looking away from the screen. Afterwards, she told Melissa she would be picking their next movie.

After the movie, Richard and Caroline got a table at Demos' in downtown Nashville. It was crowded as usual, but the tables turned quickly bringing new guests all around them. While waiting for their meal, Richard dove into the warm rolls, which were irresistible to him. The bread at Demos' was second to none. Caroline showed some restraint by having only one piece, but Richard asked for another basket when their waiter came by.

Wanting to have a serious conversation with Caroline, Richard weighed his words carefully to not scare her off. He took a drink of his iced tea before starting. Their relationship was relatively new and undefined and he didn't know how exactly to broach the subject. As he approached the topic he relived the conversation with Renée from several weeks earlier, which ironically had the same theme. His stomach sank.

"Richard, are you alright?"

"Huh? Oh yeah, I'm fine." Clearing his throat, Richard started to tell Caroline what was on his mind when the waiter arrived carrying their food. He instantly decided to postpone it until after the meal.

Richard kept the conversation light while they were eating for obvious reasons. Caroline coiled seafood fettuccine around her fork, letting it cool just a moment. "Thank you for bringing me here. I haven't been to Demos' in a very long time."

"Believe me, it's my pleasure." Richard carved into his steak. The juices coming out made his mouth water. Confident with his choice, he would wait until later to have such a serious conversation.

They declined dessert. Richard paid the check and they walked out with their stomachs full and hearts happy. But the unspoken words still loomed within Richard.

In the car driving home, Richard reached for Caroline's hand and kissed the back of it. She smiled. He never wanted to let go of that hand and longed to see years from now their aged, weathered hands still intertwined. A new territory for Richard, he finally understood the idea of growing old with someone. He wanted to grow old with her.

Placing the car in park in her driveway, Caroline glanced at her watch. Joshua would not be home for another half hour or so.

"Would you like to come in for a cup of coffee?"

"Sure."

Walking into the kitchen she asked, "I hope decaf is okay. I've been having trouble sleeping lately, so I don't dare have caffeine after three o'clock."

"So have I. Maybe I should think about switching. Funny thing, my mom can drink a cup of coffee at night before going to bed and it doesn't bother her one bit. But let her drink a glass of tea after five and she is awake all night." Caroline looked his way and giggled out loud. Her laughter was like music to his ears. Time stopped momentarily. Lessening the space between them, he wanted to reach for her, but waited until she set the coffee pot in its stand.

"I love to hear you laugh. You can brighten up a whole room with your laughter." Caroline remained speechless, but her expression said it all.

Richard stepped in even closer and took her hand in his. He could feel her breath near him. He waited to see if she would pull away, and she did not. Drawing her in a little more, Richard's lips lightly touched hers for a brief moment. After they stepped apart, they stood motionless staring at each other as time stood still when a car door shut. Joshua was home from work.

Ten minutes into work, Caroline was juggling chaos. The line up consisted of three with broken bones, two pregnant women in labor, an elderly man in severe pain, and a child with a high fever. All showed up before noon. She was responsible for collecting their information and typing it into the system. She needed to focus on these patients, but Richard and his soft kiss last evening kept playing in the reels of her mind. How was she to get any work done? Caroline had never been one to slack off at work, but today it was hard to stay on task.

The ER eventually calmed and the shift was changing. LaDonna, Caroline's co-worker, came in setting her purse down and asked how things were going. "Oh, girl, it has been a zoo around here today. I hope for your sake the night shift is not like this," Caroline explained with an exhale.

"Yeah, but it is supposed to be a full moon tonight, and you know what that means."

"Babies!" the two ladies chimed in unison as they looked at each other. She didn't envy the medical staff on days like these.

Half an hour later, Caroline signed out and headed for home. Tired and hungry, she was grateful the traffic was moving along quickly. In less than thirty minutes, she walked through her front door. After setting her purse and keys down on the entry table and losing no time in changing her clothes, she went straight for the sofa thinking she could relax for a few minutes before she would need to start supper.

Feeling her body soften and her mind slowing down, Caroline could sense sleep coming. And she welcomed it, until abruptly her phone rang and almost caused her to jump off the sofa.

"Hello."

"Hey Caroline, are you busy tonight?" Melissa asked. "I need to make a run to the mall. Want to come with me?"

"I would love to, but to be honest I don't have the energy. The hospital was so busy today. I plan on taking a hot bubble bath after supper and reclining in my chair until time for bed. I would do that right now, but I'm afraid I would fall asleep in the tub."

Joshua sat at the computer checking his messages while Caroline sat in a hot tub of lavish bubbles. The steamy lavender aroma soothed her as the day melted away. After soaking twenty minutes, she dressed for bed and wrapped a comfy terrycloth robe around herself and now desired something cold to drink.

"I'm gonna watch some TV. Wanna watch with me?" Joshua asked.

"Maybe for a little while. I was thinking of turning in early."

Caroline sat in her favorite chair in the living room drinking an ice-cold decaf tea while Joshua surfed channels until he found the station that aired back to back episodes of an old Sci-Fi show. After one episode Caroline felted her eyelids getting heavy and told her son goodnight. It didn't take long before the bubble bath worked its magic. She fell soundly asleep.

∞

Joshua turned the TV off and went to bed at ten-thirty. Tomorrow he, his uncle Curt and papaw were going fishing. He wasn't thrilled that they had to leave so early in the morning, but he would be ready or they would leave without him.

Startled out of sleep, Caroline sat straight up in bed out of breath and heart pounding. Seconds later, she realized she had been dreaming. All was dark in her bedroom when suddenly there was a loud sound that shook the house followed by a flash of light. Thunder actually woke her from her disturbing dream.

Turning on a light, Caroline got up, for a reason she could not explain, she checked on Joshua. Peeking through his doorway, careful not to make a sound to wake him, she saw her son sleeping soundly in his bed. Closing the door as quietly as she opened it, she returned to her room. Caroline sat down on the side of her bed rubbing her face with one hand. Suddenly, she sobbed uncontrollably.

❧ CHAPTER FIFTEEN ❦

Richard sat in Brian's office discussing what the day's workload would be when he decided to have that conversation that Brian knew was inevitable.

"I have something else to discuss with you."

"Sure." Brian was a hesitant to hear his brother's words. Usually when someone started a conversation like that, it meant something unpleasant.

"I agreed to come and help you only while you were laid up. Now you're back. It's time I moved on. But...I've had a change of heart and I want you to hear me out. Please?

"I told you and Dad I didn't want to work at Dunning Plumbing, and I meant that. My plan has been to leave as soon as possible. If I had not met Caroline, I would have already gone back to Atlanta. But meeting her has changed things a lot. I'm seriously thinking of staying in the area to see where our relationship goes. If it goes nowhere, then I'll return back to Atlanta. If it turns out to be something great, then she and I will both decide where we'll call home."

Brian began to speak but Richard cut him off. "Aaaand... you will not breath a word of this to anyone, or I will break your other leg."

"So, big brother may have himself a woman," Brian teased. Richard looked seriously at his brother, "Alright, I won't say a word. But tell me, are you going to take me up on my offer?"

"Not sure yet. I said I was thinking about staying in the area. I didn't say I was going to work for Dunning Plumbing."

"Rich! Why do you do this to me?" Brian whined.

"It's fun."

Richard left Brian's office and went to his makeshift cubicle, Richard's temporary office. A box of Krispy Kreme doughnuts sat on his desk; he was curious how they got there. I didn't put those there. Nor did I get myself a cup of hot coffee. He opened the box to take a look inside. Strawberry-filled...my favorite. Scratching the side of his head he walked to the receptionist, Janis, and asked if she had been responsible for the surprise.

"No sir, wasn't me, but I bet I can guess who it was."

Before figuring out the little mystery, he was detained by a phone call from Caroline that only lasted a few minutes.

Caroline and Richard had been casually dating for almost two months. If it were up to him, they would already be married and living happily ever after, but that was a bit presumptuous. In all reality his future depended a lot on her feelings toward him. Taking one of the doughnuts and stopping just as it touched his mouth it occurred to him. "I've never told her how I feel about her," he said out loud.

"Excuse me?" Thinking he was alone, he quickly turned to see Sidney standing in the doorway.

"Oh, nothing. I was just thinking out loud."

"I see you're enjoying your doughnuts," she said with a smile.

"Yes, I don't know...were these from you?"

Smiling bigger, she nodded her head.

"Thank you, Sidney. I had no idea who had put them here."

"Well, I know how much you love Krispy Kreme doughnuts and strawberry-filled is your favorite. It was just a little something to let you know how much I appreciate you and have enjoyed working for you."

Awkwardly, Richard was at a loss for words. "That was kind of you. Thank you."

"No problem. I've gotta head out to my next job, but I'll see you later." With that, Sidney left.

Richard's thoughts returned to Caroline. He remembered their conversation being odd earlier that day. She said it had been a tough day, so he figured it was just fatigue. He had a date with her that night and planned to discuss their relationship and his future with her. He did not want to push her, but he needed to know which direction his life was about to take and if Caroline would be in it.

Richard beat Caroline to her home by minutes. He was contemplating circling the block when she turned into the drive.

"I'm sorry, Were you waiting long?"

"No. No I actually just pulled in."

"Make yourself at home. I want to freshen up just a bit. I won't be long. Promise."

"No problem. Take your time."

Caroline came out of her room within a few minutes and had changed out of her work clothes. She now wore a pair of capri's and a casual blouse. She felt more relaxed, but looked a bit tired. He wondered if she felt well. Thinking fast on his feet, he had the solution.

"Caroline, sweetheart, you look tired. Would it be ok if we ordered pizza in?"

"You know, that might be best. The number is next to the phone. I think there is some Coca-Cola in the fridge." For the past couple of weeks Caroline had been supplying Richard's favorite soft drink.

While grabbing a Coke for Richard, she poured herself an iced tea. As Richard called in their pizza, it suddenly occurred to him, "I wonder if Joshua will take my order?" he asked comically while waiting for someone on the other end to answer.

"Could be."

The pizza arrived shortly piping hot so Richard tipped the delivery guy well. Caroline had plates and drinks ready when Richard sat the box on the table. Sitting in the kitchen, Richard ate without hesitation, but Caroline only picked at hers. Being a bit preoccupied with his thoughts, Richard didn't notice. He decided this would be a good time to initiate the conversation that badly needed to take place.

"Caroline, I want to talk to you seriously, if I may," he said setting his pizza down. "We have been seeing each other for several weeks now, and I have loved every moment of it. And I guess what I am trying to say is, I would like for us to talk about how we feel toward one another."

Looking at her from across the table, he paused. Confused by the look on her face, she appeared as if she was hurting.

"Caroline?" he said softly.

Avoiding his gaze, she got up and went to the kitchen sink trying to busy herself with something. Rising up out of his chair, he followed her and gently turned her around to face him. It never failed. He always got so lost in her beautiful face. And right now, even though her eyes were sad, she was beautiful. He wanted to look at that face for the rest of his days. He was sure of it, but her feelings were unknown. Closing the gap between them, he kissed her softly and asked her what was wrong.

"Richard, I think we need to stop seeing each other," she said just above a whisper as she reclaimed her chair at the table. She needed the space between them.

Richard suddenly felt as if he was in a boxing match with a prize boxer, and he just took a hard right cross to the face.

"What? I don't understand. I thought things were good between us."

Caroline choked back the tears and tried to explain. She really wanted to run away, but he deserved an explanation. She would attempt to give him one.

"They are very good. That's the problem. Richard, I cannot do this. I'm so sorry. I never meant to hurt you, but if we continue, I'm afraid later we both will be hurt worse than we are right now. It is for this reason I never wanted to get in a relationship with you...with anyone. Richard, I love the wonderful way you make me feel. I haven't felt that way in a very long time."

"What happened? Something must have happened to make you feel like this. Have I done something to hurt you? If I have, just tell me and I'll fix it. I promise, Caroline, I'll fix it."

"No, you haven't done anything wrong," she replied with deep sadness in her voice.

She looked into his eyes, his face becoming a blur until she blinked and a tear spilled over landing on the table in front of her. The kiss they shared a few days ago and the one just now had rekindled feelings she thought had died along with Craig. When Richard touched her, she wanted to melt in his arms and stay there forever, but now she knew what she had to do.

"No, Caroline. We cannot be over." The look on Richard's face told her his heart was breaking, and by the look on hers, she was in no better shape. He attempted to extract more information out of her, but it was not making much sense. It all sounded mixed up.

The only reason Richard had not spoken those three little words every woman wishes to hear is because he felt it was too soon, and he wanted her to be able to say them back to him. He couldn't deal with being in love alone. Now, words spoken or not, it looked as if he were alone after all.

⇢ CHAPTER SIXTEEN ⇣

The summer flew by and now it was the last weekend before school started. Joshua was not thrilled about returning to school, but was ecstatic about it being his senior year. He and his friends had planned a big last-weekend-before-school-starts bash. The theme for the party included friends, food, games and silliness. Dillon's injured hand had not slowed him down too much. The muscles were getting stronger and the dexterity increased each day. By the way he played video games no one would have guessed he was ever injured. Eric and Austin planned to challenge Dillon and Joshua to a championship match. Jana unfortunately was still out of town with her family and would miss the gathering. Heather showed up at Joshua's about ten minutes late bringing a surprise that threw the guys off their game.

"Hey guys! This is Natalie. She and her family just moved here." They just stood there looking at this girl as if they had never seen one before. Joshua walked in and upon seeing her, almost dropped the bags of chips he was carrying.

"Oh, Joshua, this is Natalie. She just moved here."

"Hello, where did you come from?" The voice inside his head berated him, LAME! That was sooo lame!

"We've just moved here from Georgia. My dad got a job transfer."

"Cool…aah, welcome, come in. Can I get you something to drink? We have chips and cookies and some miniature pizzas about to come out of the oven. To drink we have Pepsi and my mom has a few Dr. Peppers left in her private stash. I'm sure she won't mind if you have one."

Natalie giggled at Joshua. She wasn't making fun of him. She just thought he was cute. "Pepsi will be fine, thanks."

The other guys were now able to speak and were trying their best not to sound like an idiot like their host just did.

Walking in the living room with her drink, Natalie recognized the video game Eric and Dillon were playing.

"That's a really cool game. I just got that one a few days ago, so I'm not very good at it." Dillon, for reasons not known to man, suddenly forgot how to play. Clearly it was going to take a little time before everyone became comfortable around this new person, or at least the boys.

Caroline came out of her room to grab a cold drink and to say hi to Joshua's friends. She allowed him his space when they were there, making only brief appearances from time to time. She trusted her son and knew he had good friends, but a group of teenagers left alone with no adult supervision just seemed to spell trouble to her.

"Joshua."

Caroline called her son over to ask whom the new face belonged to, and worked hard to prevent from grinning as she listened to her son stumble over his explanation.

Richard and Renée spoke the day before over the phone, and she could tell by the tone of his voice something had gone awry. He mentioned he had an interview with a company in Atlanta and would be seeing her in a couple of days. He was unsure if he wanted the position, but if they offered the job he would probably accept it. Where he worked or where he laid his head at night no longer mattered to him. The only thing that concerned him was Caroline, but she had let him go. Just the thought of her cut him to the core. His plan was to get some sort of a job to distract and exhaust him nightly hoping that it would get her out of his mind. His heart was an entirely different matter.

Katie walked down the hall and saw Richard packing. His heartache was obvious to her, and she could feel his pain. Richard had briefly told her about his split with Caroline. From what Richard had told her she could not shake the feeling that there was something not right. It just didn't add up. He asked to not talk about it, and she would grant him that.

Shocked at how quickly Richard's situation had changed since the brothers discussed in his office the possibility of him staying in the area, Brian was even more surprised to learn how fast he had gotten an interview with a company in Atlanta.

The day had been a long one for Caroline. She had agreed to stay late to cover for a friend. Looking at her watch she realized she had one more hour to go. As always, the last hour was the longest of any situation whether work, school or traveling. Joshua would be home and would have already eaten by the time she arrived, which would make her evening a bit easier. All she wanted to do was to be at home, take a hot shower, and climb into bed.

Signing out on her computer, Caroline exhaled knowing her day was finally done. Her next task now was to go home and act like life was fine. She needed to conceal her sadness from Joshua. She would attempt to have their nightly routine as normal as possible, including the look on her face.

Even though Caroline worked at making everything look fine on the outside, inside she was dying. Neither did she have any appetite nor did she take any calls. She told Joshua to take messages and would return them later. She refused to deal with any questions or explanations. She explained to her son what had happened and that she really didn't want to discuss it any further. Respecting his mother's wishes, he let the subject drop.

"Mom, Melissa called. I told her you were in the shower, she said she would call back." he said as his mother stepped into the living room. Joshua had been honest with Melissa. Normally Caroline would return her call almost immediately, but not this evening.

"Thanks, honey."

"Mom, are you alright?" Joshua gently inquired. Immediately there was a tapping on the front door. Looking out the peephole, he called out, "It's Melissa." Opening the door, he was relieved to see her Joshua did what most men would do in this situation, he left the room.

Taking one look at her friend, Melissa knew right away something was wrong and automatically assumed it was about Richard. Just seeing her friend caused Caroline's tears to come on their own accord.

Caroline forced the tears to stop. Not wanting to rehash the whole event, she cut right to the chase "Richard and I won't be seeing each other any longer. It is at my request not his."

"May I ask why?" she said softly.

"I felt it was best for both of us and I really don't want to talk about it, Melissa," she said in a quivery voice.

"Alright. If that is what you want, it will eat you up if you keep it inside. But when you get ready, I'm here. I'll always be here for you, Caroline, just like you are for me."

❧ CHAPTER SEVENTEEN ❦

Rising early Richard had everything packed when his niece and nephew came down for breakfast. He wanted to spend time with them before they headed off to school, thankful that it was not Katie's day to drive the car pool.

Taking advantage of this, Jake reminded his uncle about his birthday.

"How could I forget?" he chuckled.

"I'm going to miss your face around here, Uncle Rich. I have to say, you're pretty cool to have around." Ashley said setting a bowl on the table to be filled with cereal.

"Yeah, I have to admit it too, I'm the coolest uncle you have." he answered with a wide grin.

Time passed quickly and soon Jake and Ashley left for the day, and also his signal to be going too.

"Russ, Katie, thank you again for letting me stay here. I can't tell you how much I appreciate it and how much I'm gonna miss you."

"Well, little brother, our home is your home. I hope you know that."

"Yeah, come back any time, man," Russ added as he slapped his brother-in-law on the back.

Nothing could be hidden from older sisters, especially when siblings were close like Richard and Katie. She could see what had happened between he and Caroline was causing him deep sorrow. He had asked not to speak of it, so she kept her thoughts to herself.

"Ok, guys, I've got to get movin'. Don't know when I'll be this way again, but I'll see ya then."

"I'll walk you out," said Katie.

Russ gave his wife a few minutes alone with her brother. She watched Richard load his gear in the back of his truck and told him she enjoyed having him around. "I don't like you living so far away."

Looking out into the distance, Richard knew he would have to tell his family sooner or later and thinking that this was as good a time as any. "It was Caroline's choice to end things, not mine. I thought everything was going well. I don't understand it, Katie. I finally find a woman that I want to have a serious relationship with and before I can tell her I love her and want to spend the rest of my life with her, she ends it."

Katie didn't know what to say to her brother to lessen his hurt. He looked so vulnerable at this moment. She wanted to wrap her arms around him and tell him she would fix it, just like when they were kids. Though she could not fix this, she could wrap her arms around him, and that is what she did. "Love ya, little brother."

Richard had said goodbye to the crew at Dunning Plumbing the day before. Four and a half months ago when all this began, Richard could not wait for this day to come. He knew it would be glorious to go back to his own home and resume his own life, but now it was bittersweet at best.

He was shocked to see how Sidney reacted to his departure. After her words and hugs, he realized her true feelings for him, for which he was happy that she had kept to herself. Everyone could tell she was holding back her tears.

He left Brian with some names and numbers of contractors and other contacts to help boost the business. Brian had been working full time for the past week and a half, and with much relief Richard had gladly turned Dunning Plumbing back over to him.

Handing Brian a piece of paper with a name and number on it, he instructed him firmly. "Here is a name you need to contact: Eric Bishop. Don't get thrown off by his age. Believe me when it comes to computers this kid knows what he is doing, and what other people are doing. He can create you a new website. And yeah, you need a new one."

"Kid? How do you know this kid?"

"Friend of a friend."

Richard exited the office with his briefcase in one hand and his coffee mug in the other.

"Renée, where are you?" Richard said to her voicemail. "Just wanted to let you know I should be at my apartment in a few hours. Maybe we can get together this week, do dinner or something. Talk to you soon." Closing his phone, he pulled into his parents' driveway.

Sitting at the kitchen table, his mom poured each a glass of iced tea and put some blueberry muffins onto a plate that had just come out of the oven. This would have been a wonderful treat had Richard felt like eating. He hadn't had much of an appetite since the fateful dinner with Caroline three days ago.

Keeping it as brief as possible, Richard explained to his parents about their breakup. Their sympathetic hearts reached out for their son. They recognized that he didn't want to talk about it and respected his wishes. Grateful for their silence, he didn't think he could say the words out loud again.

After two glasses of tea and few bites of his muffin, Richard only half listened as his dad talked about some renovations they were hoping to do to the house. Over the past few months, Richard had created in his mind a future life with Caroline. As he sat there he recalled his dream of being where his parents are now with her, but now that would never be. Letting out a sigh, he told his parents he needed to be heading out. He kissed his mother, hugged them both and repeated his appreciation speech that he had said to Katie.

On his way out of town, Richard drove by Caroline's house. As painful as it was, he could not keep from it. All was still and quiet. There were no cars in the driveway and no signs of anyone inside. The sky began sprinkling rain as he stared at the little house where he had experienced such happiness. Remembering the evening he repaired her sink, she would barely speak to him. Then he recalled their first date eating in her kitchen. The memories caused his heart to ache. All that was left to do was to slowly drive away.

∞

For the past hour, rain fell in middle Tennessee. The gray sky matched Caroline's mood. She had been at work for three hours and was having difficulty focusing. Her thoughts remained on Richard and the hurt she had caused him. His face flashed endlessly in her mind. The blame was solely hers. She had accepted his first phone call, his first invitation for a date and allowed him to hold her hand. She welcomed his kiss which stirred up her emotions. She continued to tell herself, Yeah, it's my own fault, but ending it was best for both of us. She simply wanted this to be finished so she could move forward and get back to her life as she knew it, but her mind, and her heart prevented that from happening. She relived the ballgames where he just so happened to show up and his hard earned attempts to talk to her. Then she would see his smile and those eyes. Richard had the most caring eyes. The thinking of ballgames gratefully shifted her mind to running. She needed to get back into her routine. Every year soon after the school year started Caroline began running to get back into shape for the basketball season. Being a referee meant she had to be able to run the court with the kids, and the last thing she needed was to be huffing and puffing while doing so.

Richard arrived in Atlanta around four that afternoon. Taking his time, he certainly wasn't in any hurry to get there. Just inside the door, he dropped his bags and just stood gazing around at his lonely apartment. There were no signs of life here, just empty, furnished rooms. He was glad to be in his own home again, but so much had changed. Where once his apartment welcomed him, it now just reminded him that he was alone. On the way back to Atlanta, he had lectured himself firmly. Beginning tomorrow, he was putting his life back together by starting with finding a new job.

His ringing cell phone brought him out of his thoughts. "Hey, Rich. Sorry it took me so long to get back with you. I'm glad you're back home to stay. Dinner sounds great. Let's shoot for the weekend."

"Okay, the weekend it is. I'll be busy for the next few days contacting former clients and hopefully getting another interview scheduled, the one I had didn't pan out."

"You, my friend, will find something soon. You know too many people to not get any leads."

"Let's hope you're right."

Richard and Renée ended their call with her letting him know she would stop by before the weekend. He was thankful that the two of them still had their friendship.

In three days Richard had been on three interviews. Each went well and held promise, but the ball was in their court. All he could do was wait for their call. However, in the meantime, he would schedule more interviews. He needed to work somewhere as soon as possible, not for the sake of money but for the sake of his sanity.

The long day of interviews resulted in Richard seeking the comfort of his sofa and TV. Suddenly a tapping at the door forced him to get up. It was Renée, a sight for sore eyes.

"Hey, Rich. Thought we would watch the game tonight," she said stepping over the threshold.

"Game, what game? Is there a game on, tonight?"

"Richard," she said in a stern voice. "The Braves are playing tonight…what's the matter with you?"

"Oh, yes, of course. I've had a lot on my mind."

Renée chalked it up to worry about the interview he had today. She knew from experience that interviews could rattle any person's cage.

Getting the sense that Richard was not himself, she prepared soft drinks, put some chips into a bowl while warming up the cheese dip and took their little feast to the living room.

"Aah, here it is!" Richard exclaimed. "I was about to think the network was not running the game. I hate it when they do that."

Looking at her friend, she knew something was not right. His face was drawn and pale and his eyes filled with sadness.

"Are you gonna tell me what's going on or do I have to drag it out of you?"

"Nothing. There is nothing going…there's nothing."

"Well…that cleared that up."

Richard just wanted to watch the game in silence and for a little while Renée let him until she could not stand it any longer. She knew he had been dating a woman back in his hometown and had sounded very happy in that relationship. After a little more prodding, he finally told her everything, the whole story from start to finish leaving out nothing.

Renée was absolutely dumbfounded. It didn't make any sense. This was a wonderful love story in the making. It sounded as if something or someone had interfered with their love before it was allowed to fully bloom. Richard loved this woman. She heard it in his voice and saw it in his eyes.

She wanted dearly to help heal his hurt, but the only thing she could do right now was to listen and to be his friend.

"Renée, I need to ask you something. I realized something a few days ago when Caroline and I last talked. It reminded me of one our conversations." There was a moment of silence as Richard observed his friend.

"I was that jerk to you, wasn't I?"

His words caught her off guard. She knew that he was referring to their conversation several weeks ago about defining their relationship. She responded softly.

"Yes, you were."

"I am so sorry."

Seeing Richard's vulnerability was nearly her undoing. "It's alright...I'm alright. To be honest with you, I don't think you and I could ever be as good of a couple as we are friends," she said honestly.

"Yeah, I guess you're right. I hope Stan knows what he has."

"You could tell him sometime," she teased, causing them both to laugh out loud.

Happy or not life was moving on. Joshua continued on as a busy teenager with school, friends and ball practice. Also he and Natalie had begun dating. As a mother, Caroline had covered the bases with her son over the years with certain topics that only a parent should. But when he got a little older he needed the wisdom and teaching that only a father can provide, she relied on her brother Curt, who gladly stepped in.

Saturday mornings and a few evenings after work evolved into Caroline's scheduled running routine. This usually cleared her mind, but not lately. It just gave her more time to think about Richard. She was attempting to get her life back on track, but nothing she tried worked. Melissa still didn't know the *real* reason why Caroline and Richard had parted. They chatted as often as they always had, but not about him. Caroline had stated her reason for their break up, but Melissa guessed there was more to it. They openly discussed their lives with each other, but Caroline was keeping this topic to herself.

Melissa noticed Caroline had lost weight and looked pale. She also noted that she didn't go anywhere that wasn't required. Melissa was not going to stand by and watch her friend sink deeper into despair any longer. She had given her space and time to work this out. Now it was time to intervene.

Saturday mid-morning Melissa knocked on Caroline's front door. She answered the door in ripped jeans and an old, baggy Nashville Sounds t-shirt.

"Hi, come on in. I'm cleaning out closets today, so grab yourself something to drink and come on back to my room."

With Pepsi in hand, Melissa headed into the bedroom ready to confront Caroline. Luckily Joshua was out so they could speak privately and more openly.

Her entire wardrobe was strewn across the bed as Caroline sat in the closet floor with the door wide open. She tossed out shoes, purses and other stuff that she could not decide to keep or give away. Melissa sat outside the closet on the floor near Caroline, but out of the way. She initiated the conversation with small talk, but soon realized that she was going to have to drag the details of her unspoken break up out of her.

"Alright, Caroline, enough small talk. I want you to talk to me. What happened? And do not waste our time in telling me nothing, or you're fine because I've known you since forever and you are not fine. And something did happen between you and Richard. I have watched you sink lower and lower into a state of depression for the past three weeks. Now talk to me," she said firmly with nothing but love for her friend.

"Nothing has...I'm....there really isn't anything to talk about. I just have a lot of neglected housework to do."

"Oh no. Ooooh no." Melissa said with authority. "We are going to talk about this. You need to get it out, and I'm not leaving here until you do. Now what really happened between you two? I know you sort of told me, but it really didn't make too much sense. Sweetie, I'm not wanting to know for my own curiosity, even though, I must admit, I am curious. I want to help you. Everyone can tell you are one miserable woman. And don't think for a moment that your son doesn't see it because he does." There was brief silence. Caroline knew she couldn't avoid her friend any longer. She knew Melissa was not going to let this go. She had to tell her something.

"I felt Richard was getting too serious and...I cannot commit to him. I felt it best to stop the relationship before Richard got hurt any deeper."

Melissa listened sipping her Pepsi as Caroline continued cleaning while trying to explain what happened. Caroline admitted that she had let her guard down and now two people were hurt.

"I am so angry at myself for allowing things to get this far," she said with frustration.

"Far? Sweetie, you two had barely begun."

"I should have never allowed him to call me. He asked if he could call me, and I told him yes. What was I thinking, Melissa?" she asked seeking an answer. "At first it was just a few phone calls, then out after church with some friends, then alone, and now look, look at this mess!"

After hearing this, Melissa felt partly responsible. She had been the one to encourage Caroline to not be afraid to talk to Richard, and now her friend was in despair.

"Caroline, do you love him?" Melissa asked softly. Caroline was standing in the doorway of her closet with one hand on her hip and the other hand rubbing her forehead. Painfully frustrated she turned and gazed at her friend with tears welling up. Her expression alone revealed her answer.

Melissa stayed at Caroline's for most of the day until it was time for her to head home and prepare supper for her husband. Caroline needed to do the same for Joshua. She didn't understand why Caroline could not commit to Richard, but did learn that her feelings for Richard ran much deeper than she suspected.

Another Sunday morning arrived finding Caroline unmotivated to go to church, but she did. For her it was another day of just going through the motions. Walking into church, she put on her happy face and tried to not reveal to anyone how she really felt on the inside. She assumed

Sabrina and Adam knew what had happened because Adam and Richard were such close friends. She was extremely appreciative they didn't question or treat her any differently.

After church services, her parents were celebrating their wedding anniversary with a large luncheon surrounded by family and delicious food, but Caroline didn't feel like being festive or eating. Her mother noticed her nibbling at what little was on her plate. Joshua, worried that his mom was becoming ill, turned to his grandmother for help. His grandmother simply explained that she was sad and that it took time to get over a special friend. She assured him that she was not only aware of the situation but also was keeping a watch on her.

Caroline was sitting out on the front porch swing alone while most of the family was out back playing a mock soccer game when her father came looking for her.

"Thought I would find you out here. Your mother comes out here a lot when something is bothering her. And over the years I've noticed you do the exact same thing. I don't know what it is about you women and porch swings," Zachary said sitting down beside his daughter and putting his arm on the back of the swing as the two began to gently sway. Caroline was close to her father and had grown closer after her husband died. She held a strong relationship with her mother as well, but her dad especially watched after her and Joshua as much as she would let him.

"I don't know what happened between you and Dunning, but I know you're hurtin'. Maybe if you told me about it, I can help take some of that hurt away." That was all it took for the levee to break loose, and the tears uncontrollably flowed as she turned into her father's side and cried.

Zachary held his daughter tight like he did when she was a little girl and consoled her. When the crying subsided, he took his hankie out of his back pocket and handed it to her. Drying her face and blowing her nose, she sat there staring down at her hands and began to speak.

"A few weeks ago, Richard and I were in the kitchen. I was making him a cup of coffee, and he walked over to where I was and gave me a gentle kiss on the lips. And it was alright that he did so. I welcomed it, and that is all it was. It made me feel alive again. I had not had those kinds of feelings for any man other than Craig. That night I had this dream that was so real...so...vivid." Caroline took a deep breath as she continued. "We were at the house, the three of us: Craig, Joshua and me. But Joshua was not a baby. He was the age he is now. We had been playing a game, and all of a sudden Richard shows up wanting me to go with him and Craig was asking me how I could love another man. I didn't know what to tell him. And then Richard kept calling for me to come to him and the whole time Craig was crying out to me not to leave him. Daddy, it was awful. I woke up and it was storming. And I went and checked on Joshua, then went back to bed and just cried. By the next morning I realized I had to let Richard go. I could not do this to Craig. There are times his memory burns inside me. I still love him, Daddy."

With his arm still around her, Zachary listened to his daughter pour her heart out thinking his would break along with hers. But she didn't need that right now. She needed a strong father to soothe her. Zachary quickly prayed silently to his heavenly Father for the right words to consol his little girl.

"Sweetheart, I know it has been tough being without Craig for all these years...you loved that boy deep. I truly believe he was the man the Lord had for you for all Craig's life. Now, I want to tell you something, and I want you to hear me, understand?" Caroline cuddled up into her daddy and nodded her head. "You are not being unfaithful to Craig, honey...you're not. You and Craig made a promise to each other on your wedding day, and you have kept that promise. You will always love him, but it could be that the Lord has someone new for you, someone that is here that you can share your life with. But you will need to put that love for Craig aside and let the Lord allow your heart to be given to another. I think Craig would want you to do that."

"Well, it doesn't matter now. I told Richard we couldn't see each other anymore, and now he's gone back to Atlanta."

"Too bad Atlanta is soooo far away, and we don't have any way of communicating from this far distance," he teased. These words brought a small smile to Caroline's face. Seeing this, he said, "Now, that's much better." Zachary added to his advice for his daughter. He told her to pray about the matter, and ask the Lord if she had been too hasty in her decision and to reveal how she should proceed.

Leaving the loving arms of her father and the comfort of the porch swing, Caroline went in search for some iced tea and a piece of anniversary cake.

❧ CHAPTER EIGHTEEN ❧

Sitting in her favorite chair channel surfing and eventually finding a ballgame, Caroline thought of Richard yet again. He consumed her thoughts most of the time, but this time she was working on a plan. She was constructing a way to talk to him and try to explain the reason for her actions. She felt better since sitting on the porch with her dad a few hours earlier. She worked out a strategy on how to talk to Richard. She wondered which game he was watching. Call him, Caroline, the voice inside her said. She then responded with, I could call him to just say hi. But what if he doesn't want to talk to me? After all, I'm the one who ended things, not him. Maybe I should just…

"Mom, are we out of pop?" Joshua called out from the kitchen standing with the refrigerator door open.

"Honey, I don't know."

Joshua came in the living room where his mother was sitting still flipping channels, and asked how he was supposed to watch the game without any pop to go with his chips.

"I'll have to drink tea," he said setting his bowl of chips down on the coffee table.

"Hmm, I'm sorry Joshua. Did you say something?"

Looking at his mother strangely, he answered, "Yeeeaah, we were talking about not having any pop to go with my chips. Mom, your mind is somewhere else today."

Joshua hit the nail on the head. Her mind was somewhere else. It was in the same place it had been for weeks, with no exit in sight. "I'll pick up some tomorrow when I go to the grocery."

"But you go to the grocery on Fridays. Mom, this is Sunday."

"What? Oh yes, of course it is. I meant when I go to the grocery…on Friday."

Joshua asked to have the remote. She mindlessly handed it over to him. Thinking she needed something to do, something to focus on, she reached for a book Melissa had given her about a month ago. Thinking that reading while a ballgame played in the background would be just the thing to help her relax, she opened it and attempted to read. The book was a mystery. The storyline held her attention until she got to chapter five when it became clear that the two main characters had a thing for each other. She silently steamed, *Great, Melissa, that's all I need, a book where two people find each other and fall madly in love and live happily ever after.* She tossed the book to the side with a little more vigor than she intended which caused Joshua to look away from the screen.

"Don't like the book?"

"Oh, sorry. I didn't mean to throw it, but no, I don't like the book."

Richard had accepted a job with Norman Pharmaceuticals. Within two weeks, he had logged as many hours as a regular employee did in a month. While at work, he made certain to keep himself too busy to think of anything other than work. The problem arrived when he went home. No matter what he tried, he could not stop thinking about Caroline. He found himself often speculating what she and Joshua were doing at that moment. It was about to drive him mad. Desperately needing a distraction he sought out the solace of his briefcase and worked into late hours of the night.

It didn't take long for Richard to settle back into his old routine of rising early and having Pop-Tarts and coffee for breakfast most days, followed by going to the Coffee Beanery on Sundays. The weekends when the convenience of the office wasn't available were the worst. To keep his mind off Caroline, he again poured himself into his new job.

Renée was out with her boyfriend a lot, so he was alone most of the time. He missed Katie and her family, especially in the mornings. There was a cooked breakfast most days, with the added quality time with his sister.

"Hello." Renée heard the voice she knew so well say on the other end of the phone.

"Hey, Rich. How goes it?"

"It's going fine. What about you?

"Fine. You busy this Saturday? Stan is out of town this weekend and I thought if you weren't busy, we could hang out, maybe grab something to eat."

"I'm not busy. Sounds good. Just come on over," he responded.

"I think you could use some time away from the office and your apartment. I'll see you around noon."

"Sounds like a plan I can stick to."

"Great. See ya Saturday."

On Saturday, Caroline had agreed to help Melissa remove wallpaper from her living room. Her husband, Alex, was going to be out of town on business for the weekend and therefore, decided this would be the most opportune time.

Caroline showed up wearing an old t-shirt and jeans with several holes in them and her hair pulled back in a ponytail.

"Alright girl, let's get this party started," she said without feeling when Melissa opened the door.

Caroline walked inside and stood in the room they were tackling with her hands in her back pockets wondering why Melissa wanted to do this.

"So, why are you taking this down and do you know how to take it down?" Her questions came out as one long sentence.

"I'm tired of looking at it. It's past time for it to go. I have a cousin that does this for a living, and she gave me clear step-by-step instructions."

Caroline had begun taking pictures off the wall when Melissa walked in with a funny round object in her hand.

"This little dooie is called a Tiger. You roll it on the wall to make little tiny holes in the paper. While we're doing that, I have water boiling to add to this stuff here that we will put on the wall with a paint roller," she said holding a bottle of DIF in her other hand. "Oh, and I have plenty of Dr. Pepper."

"I think we're gonna need it. Let's get this furniture moved out of the way and covered," Caroline instructed. Within two hours, the women had a good start on removing the wallpaper.

As the work continued, Caroline finally confided in Melissa about the nightmare she had about Craig and Richard. It brought tears to Melissa eyes as she listened to the turmoil her friend was going through. After all these years, she hadn't realized Caroline had not fully let Craig go. As they peeled off wallpaper, Melissa tried to encourage her to call Richard today and simply explain. There were moments where she seemed to be doing better, but there was still a deep sadness that could not be missed.

"I don't know what to say, and besides, too much time has gone by now."

"Caroline that is silly. Just tell him what you told me. Call him."

They stopped for lunch and a much needed break. After experiencing the hard labor today, Caroline decided she would never have wallpaper in her home, ever.

"Why didn't you hire your cousin to take this off?"

"Because I thought I could do it myself, and it appears we are doing a fine job."

"Well, that may be, but I bet neither one of us will be able to move tomorrow," Caroline said with a hint of humor.

After six hours, the paper was down, the walls were washed and ready to be prepped for painting, but that would have to wait for another day. Both women were exhausted.

When Caroline returned home, she drew a hot bath to soothe her tired body. Pouring in bath beads, she began to undress and considered Melissa's advice to call Richard, now. It was unusual for her to have her cell in the bathroom with her, but there it lay beside the tub. Picking it up, she scrolled down to Richard's name.

Richard worked hard at keeping his mind busy. He had spent as many hours at home working as he did at the office.

At this rate he would be up for a promotion in no time. Renée devoted most evenings and weekends to Stan, so he didn't bother her and certainly didn't want to tag along. But this Saturday, since she was free, he only worked until noon before closing down his computer. Opening the fridge he realized he had a choice to either go to the grocery or not eat in his apartment again.

Walking the aisle of the grocery store, nothing was appealing. His appetite had yet to return. He knew the supply of Pop Tarts and coffee needed replenishing. Just as he reached for the Maxwell House his cell phone rang.

"Richard, how are you?"

"Hi Katie, I'm fine. I'm at the store. I was out of coffee... and stuff."

Katie and Richard talked while he continued shopping. She guided him on a few selections of what to buy.

Without letting her brother know she was checking on him, she reminded him of Jake's birthday. It was the best excuse she could come up with without being obvious. Just the sound of her voice cheered him up. It was good to hear from her and get an update on the family. After ending his call, he walked to the cashier line and began to unload his groceries onto the belt. He instantly remembered that he had promised Jake to take him on a camping trip for his birthday.

Returning to his apartment, Richard restocked his kitchen, then poured himself a Coke. Picking up the remote he plopped down on the sofa and began to channel surf. Looking at his watch he wondered why Renée hadn't shown up yet.

An hour later, Renée knocked on the door.

"Sorry, I'm running late on everything today."

"Something to drink?"

"Sure…I can get it myself. So, tell me, what have you been doing besides work, Rich?"

"Going or coming home from work," he said dryly. "Oh great!" Richard exclaimed as he looked down and saw where he had dribbled Coca-Cola all down his shirt. "I'll be right back," as he went to change. On the way to the bedroom he heard his cell phone ring. "Get that for me, would ya?"

"Hello." There was silence. "Hellooo?" she repeated.

"I don't need to dress up for you do I?" Caroline heard Richard say in the background.

"I'm sorry I have the wrong number," the connection was cut off.

Renée didn't have a chance to tell the caller she was answering for Richard.

Caroline sat in her tub of bubbles staring at nothing, her mind trying to calculate what had just happened. It didn't take long for her to conclude that Richard had moved on and now was seeing someone else.

Coming out of his bedroom wearing a clean shirt, Richard was ready to continue his do-nothing evening.

"Who called?"

"It was a wrong number."

Relieved, he really didn't want to talk to anyone other than Renée.

Slowly with a low groan, Caroline rolled over and sat up on the side of the bed. Rubbing her face with her hands to help wake herself up, she could feel the muscles in her shoulders tighten from the simple act. She willed herself to rise and make her way towards the bathroom knowing a hot shower would probably help. Her body protested loudly reminding her of her day with wallpaper. She somehow managed to walk across the floor feeling stiff and sore.

Standing in the shower, the steam quickly filled the room. Caroline let the hot water run over her aching back and shoulders before attempting to wash her hair. The woman's voice answering Richard's phone echoed in her mind. Her curiosity overwhelmed her, who was she? She could feel her muscles starting to relax, but lifting her arms to shampoo her hair was tortuous. Feeling like she could stand there for hours letting the hot water massage her tender muscles, she made herself get out.

Walking into the church auditorium, Caroline took her usual seat in front of Adam and Sabrina. She was thankful that neither one had asked her about the situation with Richard. During the song service, the music director had the congregation shake hands. It was then Caroline took the opportunity to bring it up. "Has Adam heard from Richard?" Caroline asked Sabrina. With a half-smile she shook her head no. "I was just wondering how he was doing."

During most of the message Caroline thought about Richard. His handsome face floated through her mind. She recalled the time he sat behind her and tickled the back of her neck causing her to miss the entire message. Almost like today. She blinked the tears away as she questioned herself, was I wrong to end it? Quickly responding, it doesn't matter. He has someone else now. She needed to pull herself together. The last thing she needed was for everyone to see her run out of the room crying.

September was proving to be a beautiful month in middle Tennessee, as it almost always was. The air began cooling down and the humidity decreased making it quite comfortable. Katie and Russ were preparing to celebrate Jake's birthday, and she had invited the whole family to the festivities. Richard originally declined the invitation, but after remembering his promise, he changed his mind. He called his sister telling her when to expect him and to have Jake, and anyone else who wanted to go, ready for a camping trip when he arrived.

While talking to Renée, Richard had what he thought was a brilliant idea. "I'll be at Katie's for the weekend for Jake's birthday and I promised him I would take him camping. You know, Renée, you could use a weekend getaway. Wanna come?

"Uh, won't that be a little odd: you, me and Jake camping?" she answered with a hint of laughter. "Besides, when have you ever known me to go camping?"

Richard hoped Renée would join him for the weekend. He wasn't looking forward to the long drive alone. It gave him too much time to think, and right now thinking was disastrous. It had been over a month since he and Caroline parted. So far his workaholic therapy had worked pretty well, but when he had idle time on his hands, Richard was a train wreck.

"I'm sorry, Rich. I gotta pass on the camping thing. I mean... if it was at a hotel I could do it, but out in the woods with no hot water, and most importantly, no bathroom. That doesn't sound like fun to me. Besides, I don't think Stan would care too much for me going camping with another guy."

"Yeah, you're right. I wasn't thinking."

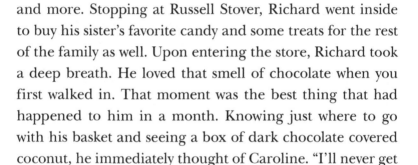

With every passing mile Richard dreaded this trip more and more. Stopping at Russell Stover, Richard went inside to buy his sister's favorite candy and some treats for the rest of the family as well. Upon entering the store, Richard took a deep breath. He loved that smell of chocolate when you first walked in. That moment was the best thing that had happened to him in a month. Knowing just where to go with his basket and seeing a box of dark chocolate covered coconut, he immediately thought of Caroline. "I'll never get over her," he muttered under his breath. Richard passed on buying anything for himself. He wasn't in the mood for sweets. He just paid the cashier and returned to his truck when suddenly it dawned on him. "I haven't bought Jake a present yet," he said out loud running his hand through his hair.

Waiting until the last minute to buy a gift was neither unusual for Richard nor shocking to anyone who knew him. But the fact that he had forgotten all about it until he thought of Caroline and the chocolates aggravated him. He needed to shake out of this fog, but for the life of him, he could not. Months ago, Caroline began consuming his thoughts. Even after they had started dating, he thought of her nearly all of the time. Currently, the only realistic change was he no longer communicated with her.

Arriving in the Rivergate shopping area, Richard made one more stop to find something for Jake before going to his sister's. Walking to the camping section in Academy Sports, Richard knew just what he was looking for. He located a tent that was neither tiny nor cheap, and then proceeded to look for a lantern. Not having children of his own, he tended to splurge when it came to his niece and nephew's.

Richard was totally focused on finding the lanterns when he physically ran smack into another person.

"Oops, I'm so sorry I was…Caroline."

"Richard."

Both had come in the same store looking for similar gear and had run into each other, literally. If it had been with their carts, it would have been one thing, but it wasn't. When Richard realized he had bumped into someone of lesser size, he automatically put his hands out to steady that person from falling. Then when he saw who it was, he quickly pulled away his hands from her as if his skin was burning. There they stood with their faces only inches apart.

"I didn't think I would be running into you today, figuratively or literally," she said trying to keep the mood light. "I'm looking for Joshua a new flashlight and …" Caroline's words sounded silly in her own ears. She was at a total loss at what to say, as was Richard. Her mind was racing, but she couldn't catch up to find any words to voice. It was as if they had entered a time warp and neither one was able to think clearly or move forward.

"Aah, yeah, I'm here picking up a birthday gift for Jake. I promised him weeks ago I would take him camping for his birthday and, well, he needed some equipment so... here I am."

"That's funny. Joshua is going camping this weekend too. He's going with a group of teens from church. Adam and a few other guys are taking them."

Richard searched for words but found none. Caroline was standing right in front of him. He could smell the sweet scent of her perfume. He longed to reach out and wrap his arms around her never to let go. He yearned to kiss her until she changed her mind about ending their relationship. But at that moment they just stood there for what seemed like hours staring at each other fumbling for things to say.

"Well, I have what I came in here for, and I really need to be getting home. Bye, Richard."

"Bye."

Richard stood blankly in the aisle watching her walk away. They were so close just seconds ago. Now she was gone and his heart felt like it had been crushed anew. He wanted to go, but he didn't know where. He just needed to go somewhere where her scent was not invading him, where he could not see her face in his mind's eye, but there was no such place.

She immediately was angry with herself. *You fool. You should have tried to explain to him why you are such a fool.* She scolded herself as she stood in line at the checkout counter. *Go, go find him and tell him you're an idiot.*

"Is this all for you, ma'am?...Ma'am?" the young cashier repeated.

"Humm, what? Oh, I'm sorry. Yes this is everything." Caroline scanned the store hoping to catch another glimpse of him among the people milling around, but could not. After paying the cashier she walked back to where they had bumped into each other only to find him nowhere in the store.

Driving home from her quick shopping trip, Caroline let the tears fall. She wanted to tell Richard she regretted ending their relationship and had made a mistake. But then she remembered the female voice on the phone. He obviously had found someone new. It was selfish to throw him away, and as soon as he found someone else, try to get him back. She had no other choice but to resume her life, just her and Joshua.

❧ CHAPTER NINETEEN ❧

The weekend with Richard's family started off poorly, seeing Caroline was like reopening a wound that was not yet completely healed. He was ready to go back home the minute he arrived, but he had promised Jake a camping trip. He would not let him down.

The day before Richard showed up Katie had a fantastic meal and party for her son and his friends. Jake was looking forward to the trip with his uncle. Richard, along with Russ and Jake's cousin Brett, were going to Fall Creek Falls to hike and camp for the next two nights. Jake was packed and ready to go before leaving for school now all he had to do was fill in the rest of the day until his uncle arrived. The campsite was a little over two hours away, which wasn't too bad since Richard would be leaving nearly right after he arrived. Jake and Brett could hardly contain their excitement.

The new camping gear was a big hit, as Richard assumed it would be. Jake and Brett were going to have a great time sleeping in it that night. Out of the car and at the campsite, Richard ordered the boys to put the tents up and then gather some sticks and kindling for the fire. The boys reacted quickly.

"So, how's the new job, Rich?" Russ asked.

"Fine, it's going fine. I've put in so many hours that I'm already ahead of the game, so it wasn't a problem taking off this afternoon."

"For someone who has a new job and is doing extremely well with it, you sure couldn't tell by listening to you," Russ commented.

"It's just a job."

"You know, Rich. It sounds to me like you are just going through the motions and not just with your job. If there is anything I can do to help, just let me know."

"Thanks, Russ. I appreciate it."

Richard fell silent as he continued to build the campfire. The boys came with arms loaded with sticks and larger logs to put on the fire. The weather wasn't necessarily cold enough for a big roaring fire, but it's part of camping and it gave Richard something productive to do. Had he been in a better mood, he would have put the boys in charge of it.

Russ unloaded the food cooler from the car and sat it nearby knowing the boys would be hungry again even though they both had a big meal just a few hours ago.

Richard nibbled on a piece of cold chicken and drank a Coke, which was enough for him. As Russ predicted, the boys ate like they hadn't had food in days. He thought his wife had packed too much food, but looking at the almost empty cooler, he knew he had been wrong.

They settled in around the fire as dusk turned to darkness. The group discussed where to hike the next day. Richard wanted to let the boys decide something themselves, and then he and Russ would figure it out.

Forgetting that his father and uncle grew up around this area and had been to Fall Creek Falls more times than they could count, Jake confidently explained the lay of the land. "There are three waterfalls you can hike to, Uncle Richard, oh and there are bat caves we can explore," he said with big eyes.

"Yeah! Uncle Richard, we gotta do the bat caves," Brett exclaimed.

Russ put a halt to the cave exploring due to a disease carried by white-nosed bats currently living in that area, which had caused the park service to restrict access to all the caves. He firmly told the boys they simply could not go in any caves. Bringing about groans and knowing Russ wouldn't budge on this, they accepted the terms.

It was about ten o'clock when Richard unzipped his tent. Looking at his phone for messages and of course seeing no signal, he closed it up. The boys were playing a game in their tent. Richard could see the movement of flashlights and hear laughter from time to time. Oh how he wished he could return to the days of his boyhood when life was carefree and easy and girls had cooties.

∞

Picking up her cell phone for the one-hundredth time, Caroline finally called Richard. "What do you mean this number is not in service?" she said aloud in her bedroom. "Well, of course not, he probably can't get a signal where they are camping." Caroline concluded feeling foolish and defeated at the same time. Foolish for thinking there would be phone service in the wilderness, and defeated for finally mustering up the courage to call Richard and explain her actions and not being able to do so. First thing Saturday morning, Caroline would do the next best thing.

∾

Caroline knew exactly who to seek out for help in this situation.

"You want to what?"

"I know it sounds silly, but, Melissa, I just need to talk to him. And I can't call him because there is no service in the woods. And I...don't know what else to do."

"Caroline, sweetie, you're not thinking. First of all do you even know where they're camping? I mean, how would we find them once we got there?"

Caroline hadn't considered that. She was so aggravated with herself. Her head was jumbled. She had a chance to talk to him in the store and blew it. Now she was faced with not calling him or going to him. Connecting with him seemed far-fetched. Maybe this is the Lord's way of telling me Richard and I should not be in a relationship, she said from an internal whisper. Clearly her mind and heart were conflicted.

Caroline's misery was apparent to Melissa and standing back watching her try to solve it was painful. She knew she needed to help her.

"May I suggest you call Katie and ask when the guys will be returning and if it would be alright if you came over so you and Richard could talk."

Caroline thought about it for a moment, and then thanked her friend for coming up with a marvelous plan that made complete sense. "Joshua. I have to pick him up at five o'clock. What if the guys all get back at the same time? Then what?" she said with slight panic.

"Then I will go pick up Joshua for you," Melissa said simply.

It was all settled. Joshua would be back at Adam and Sabrina's by five, and Richard and his group would be back by four. Caroline worried that an hour wouldn't be enough time to talk to Richard, so Melissa was picking up Joshua giving her friend all the time she needed.

The afternoon passed at a snail's pace until Caroline needed to leave for Katie and Russ' house. Caroline nervously paced the floors like an expectant father. She didn't want to get there before they returned, so her timing needed to be right on when she left. She confronted a possible reality, What if he tells me to go away? He should. I don't deserve a second chance. Caroline's nerves were frayed. Along with the endless pacing from room to room, she changed her outfit three times. Finally her uncontrollable thoughts were smothering her. She eventually relented and sat at the kitchen table waiting for the hands on the clock to tell her when to go and looking at the very spot she stood in Richard's arms and felt his gentle kiss.

Russ, Richard and the boys pulled up to the house around four-fifteen. Judging by the looks of the boys and how dirty they were, they had had a great time. The men looked a little rough, but they were smiling. Katie was relieved to see that Richard had enjoyed himself. Russ told the boys to unload the truck and they did so without complaint. Katie, in the meantime let Richard know gently that he had a visitor due to arrive any minute.

"And who would that be?" he said unsuspected with a laugh.

"Caroline." His face went somber. Before he could react, she pulled into the driveway. Russ and Katie headed into the house to give them privacy.

With hands in his pockets, Richard walked slowly toward Caroline's car as she turned off the engine and got out. Wishing for a shower before seeing her, he was covered in dirt with a two- day beard and probably smelling no better. She on the other hand was a vision of loveliness. Wearing jeans, a stunning dark blue blouse and sandals with her hair loosely falling over her shoulders, Caroline caused Richard to nearly come unraveled. His mind pleaded, why are you here? Can't you see what you do to me? She had ended their relationship now she was taunting him with her presence.

"Richard, I called Katie and asked if I could come over. I just want... need to talk to you. She said it would be ok." A silence hovered between them as she peered into his eyes. "Is it alright, Richard? Would you rather I left?"

"No." Richard was at a loss of how to respond. He really didn't want her to leave, but her being so near him was torturing him. This woman had turned his world upside down. Leaning against her car with his arms folded and ankles crossed, he looked calm and in control, but nothing could be further from the truth. A much different scene played out within his mind. His version began by taking her by the arms and slightly shaking her saying, Can't you see that I love you to the depths of my very soul? Don't you know

I can't eat, I can't sleep and all because you have invaded every piece of me? Instead he listened to her respectfully, needing to get away from the spell she had over him, but unable to move.

"Richard, I made a horrible mistake. Remember the evening you came over and we had supper alone at my home, and we had our first kiss right before Joshua came in?"

"Yes, I remember."

Richard listened intently to Caroline explain the nightmare she had that evening and the torment it caused her. He fought the urge to step out and wrap her in his arms to shield her from any hurt, no matter the source. He never thought for a moment when she told him weeks ago she could not do this that it was due to her late husband. With a shaky voice Caroline continued her explanation.

"Deep down I felt like I was being unfaithful to Craig. And after talking to Daddy he explained to me that was just not true."

As Caroline spoke, Richard remained silent. She feared her words were ineffective, but she continued.

"He explained to me that I had kept the promise I made to my husband in our wedding vows, the promise to love and be faithful to Craig until death parted us...and death did part us. But there was a part of me that had never fully let him go." Richard could see a deep sadness in her eyes as she exposed her vulnerable emotions. "He told me some other things, but the bottom line is this, and I hope you believe me. Craig was my first real love and he will always be a part of who I am, but over the past few weeks I've had to let him go. I believe the Lord has given me someone new to love and share my life with. And I believe that someone is you,

Richard." Touching his face, she added, "I hope I haven't totally destroyed that."

He took his hands out of his pockets and came off her car to full height. "What are you saying, Caroline?"

"I'm saying that I have fallen in love with you and I want you in my life."

Richard reached for her, slowly pulling her close to him and she went willingly. Standing very near to one another, she could feel his breath on her face.

"Caroline, I have loved you since the day we met."

Gently touching his unshaven face, she let her hand brush over the stubble. With his hands on her waist, he pulled her in tighter to him and kissed her with all his love. She wrapped her arms around his neck, not wanting to let him go. This was the position Russ found them in when he went to retrieve his hat from the truck.

"Ooops," he said at a whisper. Turning around quickly, he decided his hat wasn't that important.

"But what about your new…friend?" Caroline asked.

"What new friend?" he asked, a confused look clouding his face.

"I called you several days ago, and a woman answered your phone. What will you tell her?" she asked in fear of the answer.

"I don't have a clue who you are talking about. And I assure you I don't have a new…friend. Exactly when did you call?" After a little more inquiry, it occurred to him.

"That was probably Renée. She and I are just old friends", he said with a big grin, "and I can't wait for you two to meet."

As children, Katie and Richard would spy on each other to learn whatever they could, without giving it a second thought. Now, as a grown, respectable woman Katie would not think of doing such a thing, but right now her curiosity was about to get the best of her. She was anxious for Richard to come in and share some details, or at least give her a clue of the outcome of his and Caroline's long visit out in their driveway. Russ's look on his face when he came back in made Katie even more curious. Then finally, the kitchen door opened and the two walked in hand in hand, Richard looking as happy as he did that day on the lake.

❧ EPILOGUE ❧

Richard, always an early riser, had trouble getting out of bed on this particular day. He looked over to see the most beautiful woman he had ever laid eyes on asleep beside him. Caroline, his Caroline. It was hard to believe it had been an entire month since Zachary Weber placed his daughter's hand into his own as they pledged their love for one another before God, close family and friends at the Marydale Bible Church altar. With his new position at Dunning Plumbing, he and Caroline were living happily ever after. Even though Joshua had started his first year of college, Richard made it clear to him this was his home too, and he would always be wanted here.

Like his father, he now went to church to learn more about God and to worship the Lord, instead of hoping to see the woman that had caught his eye. No, this day he would lie here and watch his wife slowly wake to a brand new day. After all, there could be nothing better awaiting him than what he had at this moment.

Reba Stanley © 2014

Biblical quotations from the KJV and the NIV

Editors: TBM, M.M. Smith

Research Consultant: Brad Montgomery

Military consultant: Michael Davis, Master Sergeant (Retired) U.S. Air Force

Synopsis

Life was going just the way Richard Dunning had planned since college, making good money and living the bachelor's life.

Suddenly and without warning it all changed and Richard was not only out of a job but on his way back to his home town in middle Tennessee to help his brother who had met with a serious accident. He agreed to help his younger sibling, but he didn't agree to have his world turned upside down. After attending what was sure to be a lame high school reunion Richard knew his life would never be the same.

❧ ABOUT THE AUTHOR ❧

Reba Stanley grew up in Muhlenberg County, Kentucky, where she developed a life-long love of the arts and first came to know her Savior Jesus Christ. Reba is also a professional artist who has worked in various mediums of paint and color. She says her visual artwork is, and always will be, in her blood, but writing is the form of art she has found to be the most rewarding. With her writing, she expresses different stories that are fictional; but she always adds one unchanging truth: a love for and dependence on her Lord and Savior, Jesus Christ.

Reba and her husband of more than twenty-five years reside in beautiful Brentwood, Tennessee, with their four children and the family dog. While the Lord has taken them to live in other areas of the country, Tennessee is her home.

"Because your love is better than life, my lips shall glorify you" (Psalms, 63:3 NIV).

www.rebastanley.com

Other books by Reba Stanley:

The Garland Series
> *Storms*
> *The Rancher*
> *Where My Heart Lies*